THE STUPENDOUS SWITCHEROO

ALSO BY MARY WINN HEIDER

The Mortification of Fovea Munson

The Losers at the Center of the Galaxy

ALSO BY CHAD SELL

The Cardboard Kingdom

The Cardboard Kingdom: Roar of the Beast

The Cardboard Kingdom: Snow and Sorcery

Doodleville

Doodleville: Art Attacks!

THE
STUPENDOUS
SWITCHEROO

NEW POWERS EVERY 24 HOURS

MARY WINN HEIDER & CHAD SELL

ALFRED A. KNOPF | NEW YORK

THIS IS A BORZOI BOOK PUBLISHED BY ALFRED A. KNOPF

This is a work of fiction. Names, characters, places, and incidents either are the product of the creators' imagination or are used fictitiously. Any resemblance to actual persons, living or dead, events, or locales is entirely coincidental.

Text copyright © 2023 by Mary Winn Heider and Chad Sell
Cover art and interior illustrations copyright © 2023 by Chad Sell

Knopf, Borzoi Books, and the colophon are registered trademarks of Penguin Random House LLC.

Visit us on the Web! rhcbooks.com

Educators and librarians, for a variety of teaching tools, visit us at RHTeachersLibrarians.com

Library of Congress Cataloging-in-Publication Data is available upon request.
ISBN 978-0-593-42730-9 (trade)—ISBN 978-0-593-42731-6 (lib. bdg.)—
ISBN 978-0-593-42732-3 (ebook)

The text of this book is set in 12.5-point Sabon.
The illustrations were created using Clip Studio Paint.
Interior design by Michelle Cunningham

MANUFACTURED IN CHINA
10 9 8 7 6 5 4 3 2 1
First Edition

FOR JORIN, WHO IS JUST SUPER

–M.W.H.

TO MY MOTHER, PATRICIA

–C.S.

So, it wasn't, like, a TOTALLY normal morning.

My bunny slippers were FLYING.

Somehow, in the middle of the night, Harvey and Roger went and got superpowers. Or that's what I thought—until I lifted my arms and realized . . .

It wasn't my *slippers*!
It was *me*!

CHAPTER 1

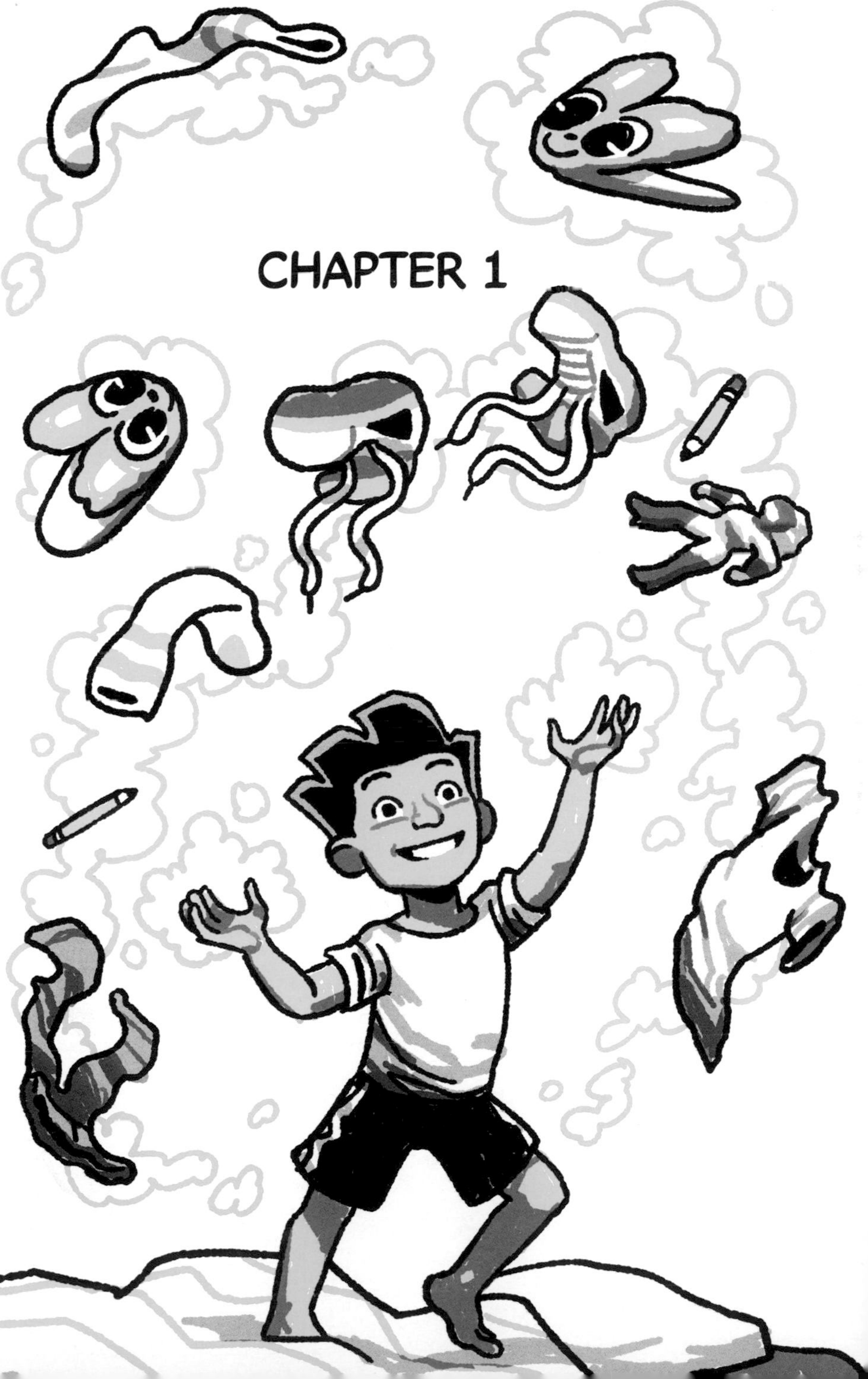

I have superpowers?

I HAVE SUPERPOWERS!

And wait, if I have superpowers, does that mean I can be . . . a superhero??????

I AM SO PREPARED FOR THIS.

I've read *every single* Vin Valor comic book.

Vin Valor

Also Vin Valor

I've watched him on *every single* news show.

I've learned everything there is about being a hero from him!

Heck, I've even written comics *myself* about Vin Valor and his genius tech inventions. I've imagined about a bazillion times that he calls me up and needs my help. And in my imagination, I have superpowers and I'm the best sidekick ever, and then people write comics about *me,* too.

It was a good daydream.

I just never thought it would actually happen!

That's when I notice myself in the mirror. I . . . *do not* look like a superhero. I look like a kid in pajamas. Vin Valor's DEFINITELY not going to take me seriously in my pj's.

I need a superhero costume!

PRONTO.

I stick my head in my closet and immediately wish that I had more interesting-looking clothes. Okay. I have to think bigger.

I suppose I *could* do something like Vin Valor—except since I'm not a tech genius, I don't just happen to have a jet pack with rocket thrusters and extension cuffs that make tools and weapons appear in an instant.

Plus, I'm not great at the technology I DO have.

(You should see what I did to the toaster yesterday.)

Or else I could be like the Granite Woman!

Since she was made of stone, she just wore some very cool armor to stop people from blasting her into pebbles.

How heavy is armor again?

OR I could be all
moody with my costume,
like Manny Mystery.

Back when he and the Granite Woman and Vin
Valor worked as a team, Manny Mystery was known
for appearing and disappearing (mysteriously, of course).

Total tripping
hazard

Considering how often I trip over my shoelaces, I
should probably stay away from long cloaks.

But maybe . . . a simple cape?

And I know exactly where the perfect cape is!

Ooooohhh. *Telekinesis.*

"Yes! That's what I've got! And I'm going to be a superhero! I just have to find a cape and I'm pretty sure there's something in the dirty laundry—"

Al interrupts me. "That's not a good idea."

"Well," I say, "maybe we can wash it first to make sure it doesn't smell bad."

"Not *that*," Al says. "I mean—I think you should consult Mom before embarking on any superhero adventures."

Sometimes living with a robot is a real pain.

Al's built-in phone rings while I throw on the cape (technically a pillowcase) and check myself out in the mirror. Hmm. Something's missing. A mask! I need a mask!

"No answer," says Al.

"Why don't you try her hovercar?" I ask, cutting a mask out of one of my socks.

"No answer there, either," Al grumbles.

"Well, I'm not going to wait around for her!" I say. "How does this look?"

Er . . .

If we wait for Mom, maybe I can make you a costume with a little more . . .

pizzazz.

"I *have* pizzazz," I say. "And look at it this way—if we can't reach Mom, she can't say no, right?"

"I do not like that argument," Al huffs.

"I'll just go on one teeny, tiny adventure," I say. "Teeny. Tiny."

Al still looks unconvinced. "You should eat breakfast first. It's better to make decisions after breakfast."

I watch Al roll off toward the kitchen—and then I run in the opposite direction. If I'm going to be a superhero, I'll need something from Mom's lab.

I push the door open and hesitate for a second. It's so quiet. It almost feels like I shouldn't be here. I mean, I'm *allowed* to be in Mom's lab. Just to be clear, I am totally allowed in here.

I'm just not supposed to touch anything.

I'm *especially* not supposed to touch anything when she's away on one of her important top-secret research trips.

She goes on top-secret trips a lot. It's not too surprising when you consider that she's probably the greatest scientist in the whole world. She doesn't like to say that—she'd say it was bragging—but it's true. She can basically invent stuff in her sleep, and she comes up with a brilliant invention approximately every two seconds.

Including the brilliant invention I'm looking for right now.

Looking for *without* touching anything.

It takes me a minute, but finally I see it, hovering over her desk with a bunch of office supplies. It looks *almost* like a regular watch—but I know it isn't.

I very carefully let everything else float back down, and then I strap Mom's backup Pinpointer onto my wrist. Now I'll be able to teleport *anywhere on Earth* for superhero missions. And when the mission is over, I can teleport right back! It's a definite perk of having an inventor for a mom.

And then something else hits me. I bet Mom can figure out why I have these powers! Right now, all I know is that I woke up this way. And I can't think of anything weird that might have happened last night.

I mean, *extra* weird. Because, okay, lots of basic weird stuff happens around here.

But I'm sure Al would have pointed out if something was *extra* weird, and instead, it was a very chill night.

Al was particularly proud of the bathtime situation.

And now, poof, I have powers!

It's a huge mystery, how all this happened. But I can confidently say that now I can move stuff with the power of my mind, and also, I smell like bubblegum.

The good thing is, I can use my powers even if I don't know how I got them! I take a deep breath, and head to the kitchen to convince Al that I need to be a superhero today. When I get there, I realize Al must be pretty worried—there is a ridiculous amount of breakfast on the table.

"You're just being a worrywart," I say.

Al huffs, but doesn't argue.

"The Granite Woman is retired, and Manny Mystery disappeared for good," I say, thinking out loud. "But Vin Valor's in the news all the time, so he's probably hard to get in touch with unless you're the president—wait! I bet Valor Technologies has a hotline! Al, call the Valor Technologies hotline!"

Al frowns.

"Please?"

With a defeated look, Al mumbles, "Mom says Vin Valor's overrated, and I don't know why you'd want to call him since *she* doesn't take *his* calls, but okay."

Thank you!

Wait, **what**? Mom's not taking his calls?

They **know** each other???

It's ringing.

Hello, this is the Valor Technologies hotline.

"I have superpowers!" I say, getting right to the point. "Does Vin Valor need any help today?"

For a minute I'm not sure if the person is still there, but then she says, "Fine. But ONLY because there's no one left here for backup and we have a situation. Give me your email—I'll send the coordinates."

Heck yeah! The moment we hang up, I run through the house, Al close behind me.

I never thought I'd actually get to MEET Vin Valor! Mom says everything in the comics isn't true and I have to remember that's not what it's really like to be a tech scientist, but I think he's awesome.

And seriously—what's the deal with her not taking his calls? Maybe he wants her to come work at Valor Tech? That would be amazing. Maybe if I become Vin Valor's sidekick, Mom might consider it???

I step onto the teleporter platform, so excited I can hardly stand it.

And then all my excitement is immediately crushed by one extremely overprotective robot.

"No way," Al yells, rolling into the room. "Mom says you aren't supposed to teleport by yourself."

"That rule is for the *old* me. Mom doesn't know about my new superpowers!" We have a short stare-off. Then I add, "Please."

Al doesn't budge.

"Come on," I say. "I never go anywhere. What could go wrong?"

Well, I guess . . .

YOU COULD ACCIDENTALLY TELEPORT INTO **THE SUN.**

I would get in a lot of trouble, you know.

"I won't end up in the sun," I say, trying not to roll my eyes. "I'll be responsible. I have the coordinates. I have Mom's backup Pinpointer."

Al thinks for a second, then sticks out a hand.

"What?" I ask.

"I need to inspect that Pinpointer."

Al makes a reluctant beep. "If you're going to teleport—

--you're going to have to follow some *rules*.

AL'S RULES

No teleporting willy-nilly!

No teleporting anybody but yourself!

You can go to *one* set of coordinates that I'll approve.

The Pinpointer will let you come back here at any moment . . .

. . . but with parental controls on, you can't go anywhere else.

I can handle a few measly rules . . . I just hope Vin Valor never learns about any of this!

"Now, let me look at those coordinates," Al says . . .

. . . And then reads *so slowly* I think I might be an old man before this trip actually happens. WHY IS IT TAKING SO LONG?? I'm going to miss all the action!

Finally, *finally,* Al enters the coordinates into the teleporter. I push the GO button on the Pinpointer. There are a few beeps. Then . . .

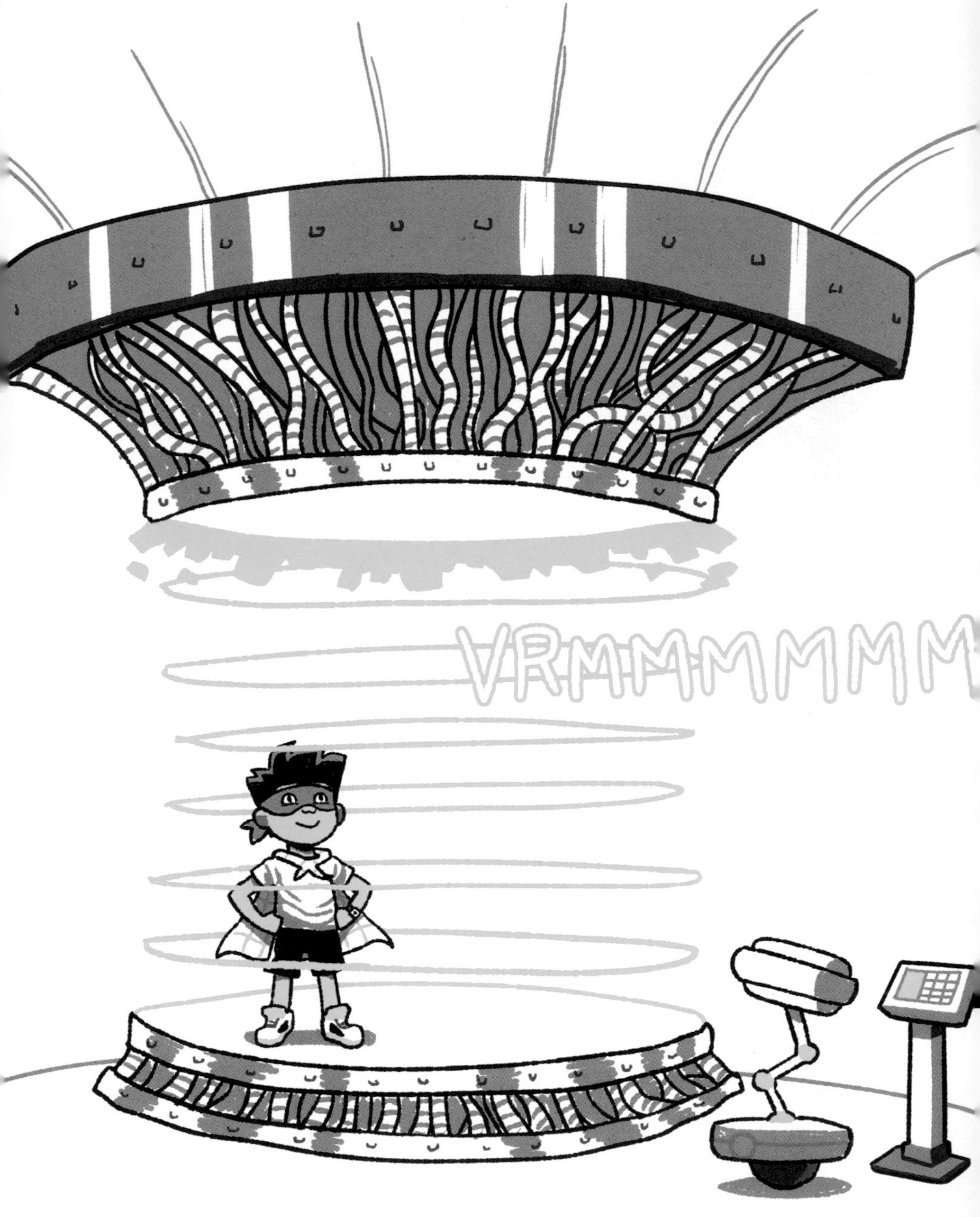
VRMMMMMMM

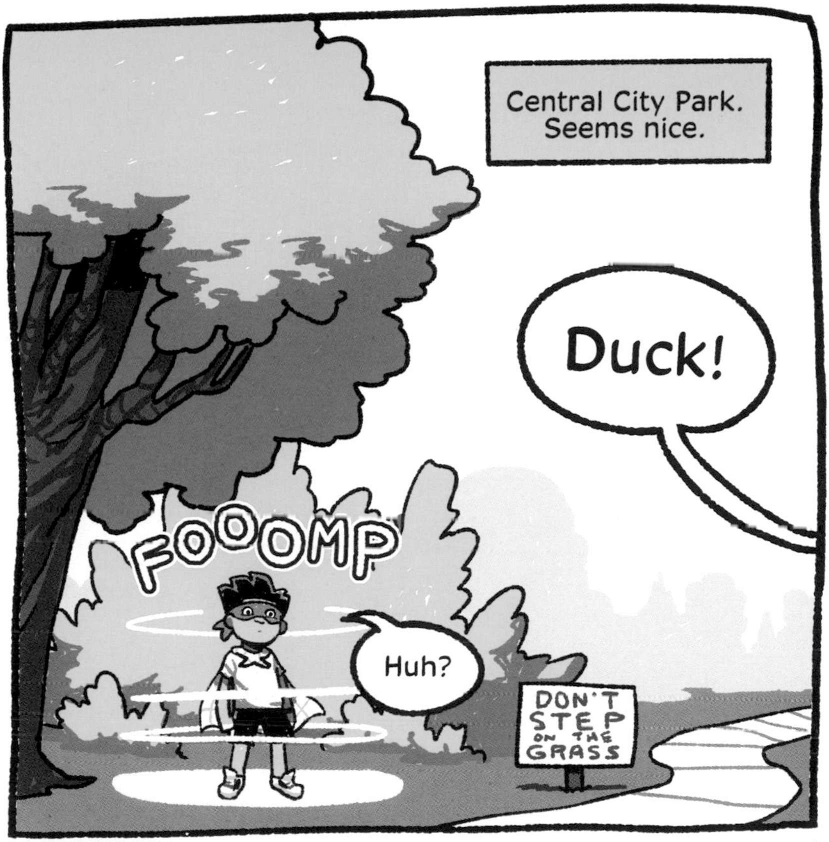
Central City Park.
Seems nice.
Duck!
FOOOMP
Huh?
DON'T STEP ON THE GRASS

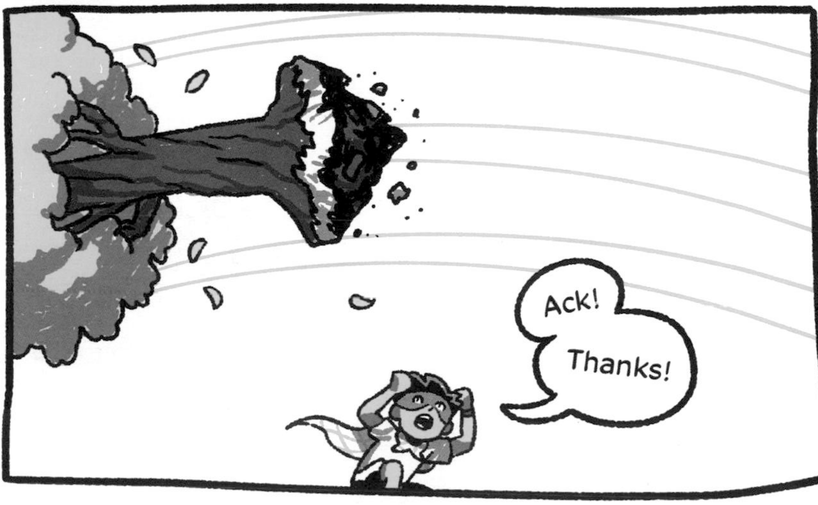
Ack!
Thanks!

Guess I didn't miss all the action!

I look around and spot a kid about my age . . . but she's flying a hoverjet and wearing an official Valor Tech jumpsuit! Maybe she's the one I talked to on the phone? And somebody else is throwing trees through the air? What is going on??? This is a weird emergency.

I'd know that blob anywhere! It's Lou Ooze! He's
a villain in the Vin Valor comics. AND HE'S RIGHT
HERE!?!?

There's a cluster of drones flying around, and as I watch, one of them spits out a net. I'm betting they're going to use it to capture him—until Lou Ooze throws a bench right into the middle of the cluster, knocking most of the drones out of the air.

The drones look wrecked . . . but I wonder if the net's still okay?

I focus hard, using my telekinesis to lift the net up and over Lou Ooze. When I pull my hands down, the net goes down too, trapping him underneath. He pushes against it, but he can't get free because I'm stronger.

Then, just when I think it couldn't get any more awesome, there's a sort of rocket-engine noise.

VIN VALOR!!!! IN REAL LIFE!!!

I want to say hi, but I can't seem to speak, plus I get so distracted I forget that my telekincsis is supposed to be doing two things at once. The net stays on top of Lou Ooze, but I crash straight to the ground.

It's not the *best* first impression.

"What happened here?" Vin Valor hovers over and points at me. "Who are you? AND WHERE DID YOU GET THOSE POWERS?"

I suddenly realize I did not plan this far ahead. Meeting Vin Valor for real and in person is making me VERY sweaty. "Um . . . hi . . . big fan . . . ," I stammer. "I'm . . ."

Vin Valor and the kid in the jumpsuit exchange a glance.

I can feel my sidekick opportunities evaporating.

"The Amazing Mover," I blurt out, instantly realizing that I have come up with the worst superhero name in all of superhero existence. Then, of course, I double down. "I'm the Amazing Mover."

"And I have no idea how I got my powers," I admit.

He studies me for a second, then breaks into a huge smile. "Well, thanks for your help today! Tana, let's make sure we know how to find him?"

Before I can say the word *sidekick*, though, Vin Valor turns to the kid. "And, Tana, clean up the Vrones? I'll see you back at HQ."

He hoists up Lou Ooze and he's about to take off when he glances back at me, like he almost remembers something. Maybe he'd been thinking just this morning how much he needs a new sidekick????

But then he's gone.

Without another word.

And OH NO HE THINKS MY NAME IS THE AMAZING MOVER.

I guess that could have gone a *little* better.

The VTech kid starts collecting the scattered Vrones from under bushes and rubble. All around us, the park is totally destroyed. There are upside-down trees everywhere. The gazebo is smashed. It's going to be a while before anybody can have a picnic here.

And then I realize . . . what if this is something *else* my power is good for? Maybe I can help fix things.

Gazebo...

unsmashed!

"Not bad," says the girl, startling me. "Usually, I use the Vrones for cleanup, but you're a lot faster."

Um . . . I am definitely NOT turning red under my mask.

"And thanks again for your help with Ooze," she says as she tinkers with a Vrone. "He might've gotten away if you hadn't been here."

"Soooo . . . are you Vin Valor's sidekick or something?" I get ready to be jealous.

She snorts. "I'm nobody's sidekick. I'm the top student at the Valor Innovations Academy this week. For the last *seventeen* weeks, in fact, and according to my plan, the top student until I graduate. It means I run the emergency line so that Mr. Valor can focus on research and development. It's like I'm a very important intern?" She sticks out her hand. "Tana Gregorio."

"So what happens now?" I ask.

"Oh, Lou Ooze goes straight to the new Valor Tech super jail," Tana says, setting the last Vrone upright. "The jail isn't even officially open yet—it's part of the new VTech business model. Villain collection."

"Ha! Collecting villains. That makes it sound like a hobby." *Super* casually, I add, "Maybe I can tag along with you to HQ?"

She frowns. "Headquarters is a secure facility. I can't bring you there."

"We put an actual real-life villain named Lou Ooze in super jail!" I crow. "Me and Vin Valor and a very important intern named Tana Gregorio!"

"Why does this Lou Ooze belong in prison?" Al asks.

"Because he's a *villain*. Obviously."

Al should really read more comic books.

I spend the rest of the day in the breakfast nook, making plans. I'm a for-real superhero now. And I need to act like it.

Which starts with a REAL costume.

I also just started this Epic Superhero Journal.

Mom and I used to do this stuff together: she'd write in her research journal and I'd draw comics. We haven't done it lately, because of all her research trips, but this way, when she *does* come home, I can tell her every single detail.

Being a superhero doesn't feel like I thought it would—everything isn't magically perfect. I mean, I fell on my face right in front of *Vin Valor*!

On the other hand, I captured Lou Ooze! So maybe there's still a chance I could be part of Vin Valor's super team someday? I hope so. But no matter what, I've got the power to help people—and I can't just ignore that.

So, welcome to my Epic Superhero Journal, with art by yours truly. What an awesome day. I can't wait for tomorrow!

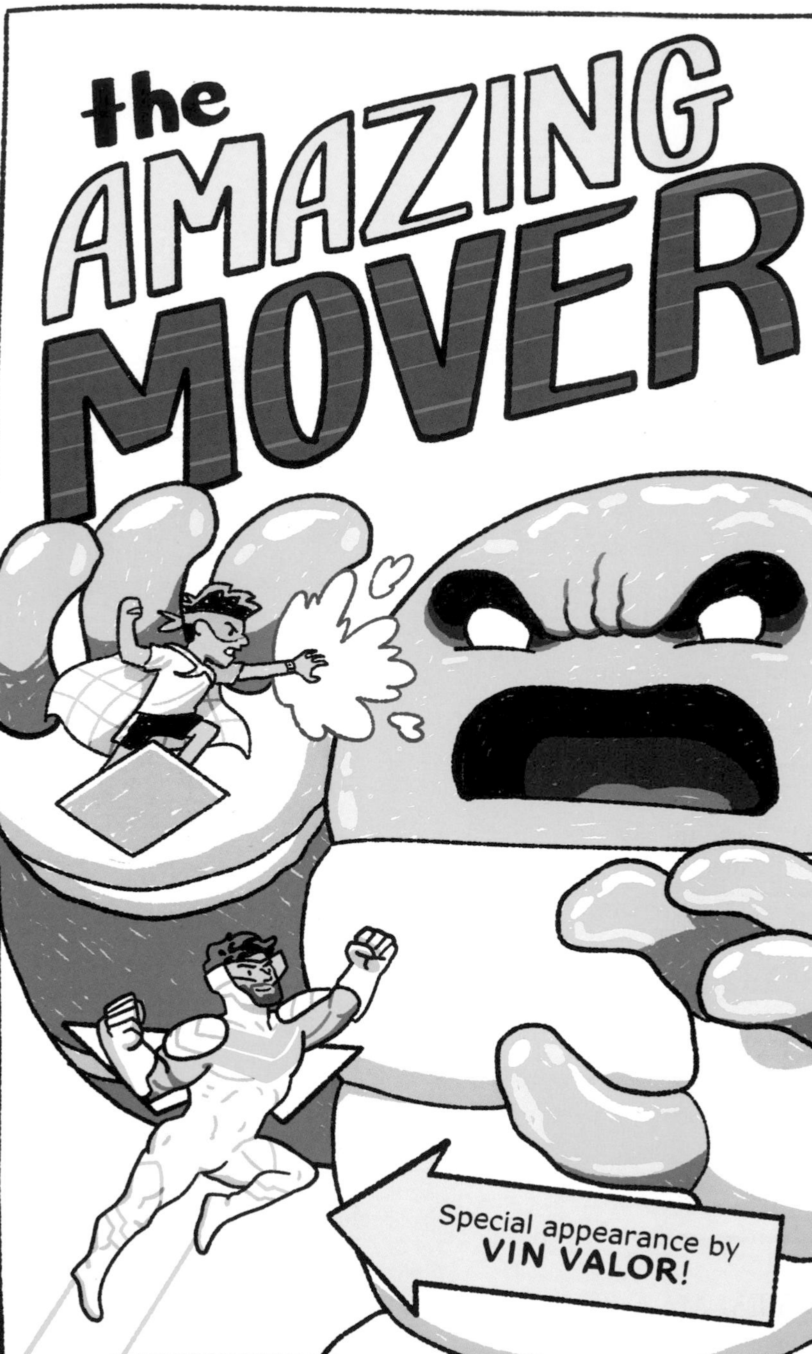
the AMAZING MOVER
Special appearance by
VIN VALOR!

CHAPTER 2

The next day starts with me having a very realistic dream about a noisy microwave. As I wake up from the dream, I realize the beeping is coming from Al, who's standing at my door.

YES! My new super suit!

This is going to be great!

I have my whole day planned: I'm going to eat breakfast, go fight some supervillains, maybe even save the world. NBD.

But first things first. I reach out, mentally speaking, and use my superpowers to put on my bunny slippers. Or at least, I *try* to.

That's when I first notice the trouble.

My slippers just sit there. Ignoring me.

Um... helloooo?

Harvey?

Roger?

I try to move other stuff in my bedroom, and nothing even budges. My superpower's glitchy. Is that a thing?

I get out of bed anyway, put on my super suit, and discover that at least one thing is going well.

I look *awesome*.

I tell Al all about the problem with my not being able to move anything.

"Maybe you should eat some prunes," Al says.

Sometimes I think Al is actually trying to get on my nerves.

I head to the kitchen and eat some prunes anyway, just in case, and then I eat some cereal, too, because I *am* pretty hungry. What if I was just running on empty?

When I finish breakfast, I focus, really hard, on the closest thing: a bunch of bananas. Very ripe. Very peel-able. I can do this.

Nothing happens. I didn't think about it yesterday, but I don't have the first clue how superpowers work—except I guess it's not related to being hungry. So . . . what? Do they have to warm up? Did I use too much power and so now I need to recharge?

I know my mom could figure it out, but when we call her again, she *still* isn't picking up.

"Al," I say. "Is there anything you can do to see if I still even *have* powers?"

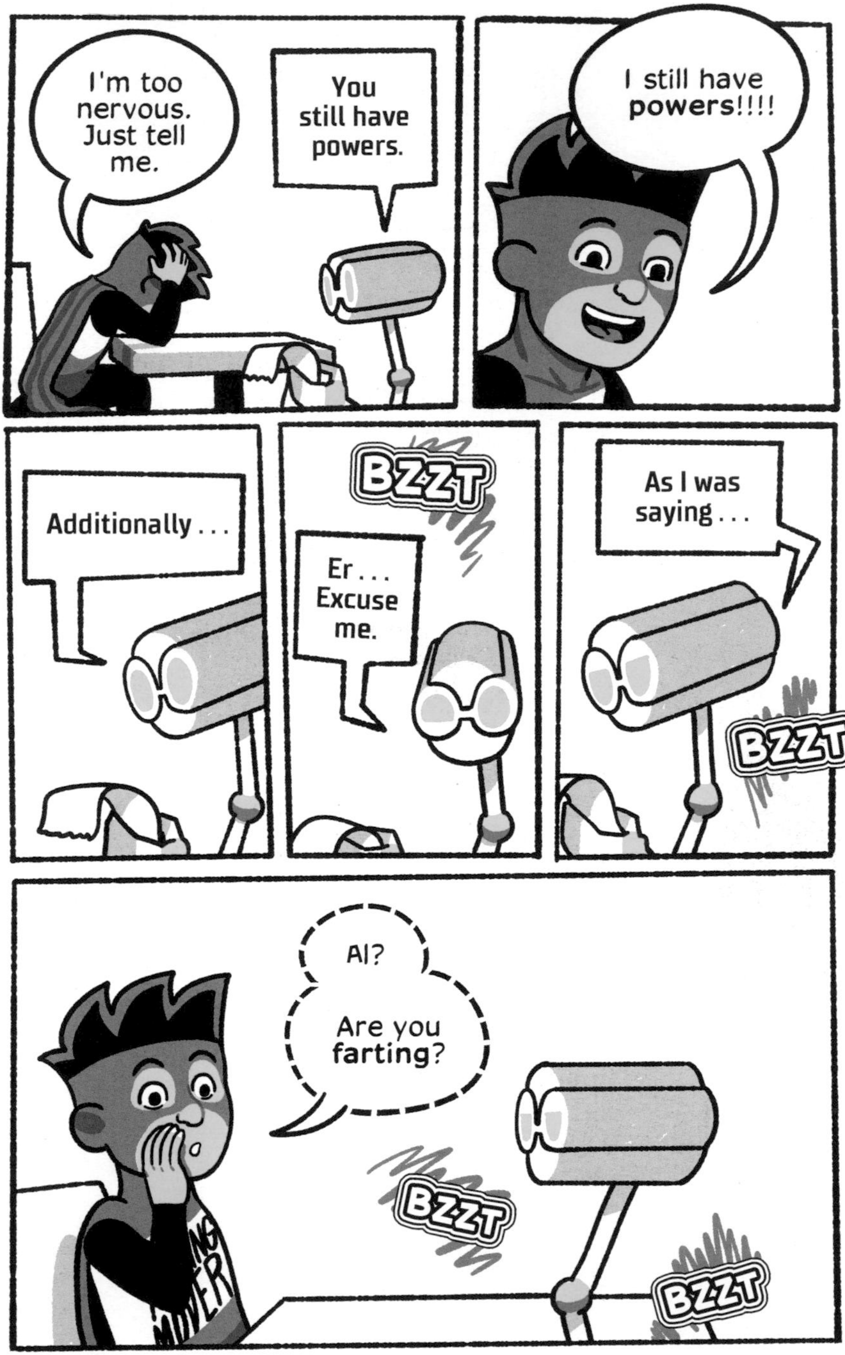
I'm too nervous. Just tell me.
You still have powers.
I still have **powers**!!!!
Additionally . . .
BZZT
Er . . . Excuse me.
As I was saying . . .
BZZT
Al?
Are you **farting**?
BZZT
BZZT

"No! That's the ringer for my hologram function. I am not farting," Al says with disdain. "I do not fart."

Al doesn't fart? How did I never know that?

As far as I'm concerned, that is *extremely* tragic information, but before I can give Al my condolences, there's suddenly a hologram in the middle of the kitchen.

Holy cow! It's Vin Valor's ~~sidekick~~ intern! Calling me! At my house! On my robot!

"Hi there," I say, trying to play it cool.

"We have a situation, and Mr. Valor suggested that you might be available to help on-site. Can I tell him you're free?"

THEY NEED ME NOW. This is incredible. I can tell Al doesn't approve, but Vin Valor invited *me* onto a superhero-type mission, and it is literally everything I have ever wanted.

". . . want to change them?" says Tana, interrupting my thoughts.

"Sorry, I . . . had a bad connection," I manage. "Change . . . um . . . what?"

I ask her to send over the coordinates, and after a quick nod, she signs off.

"We weren't quite finished discussing your powers," Al starts, but I don't have time to sit around discussing my powers! I need to go be heroic! I run to my room, grab my shoes, and then head for the teleporter, where, of course, Al is waiting impatiently.

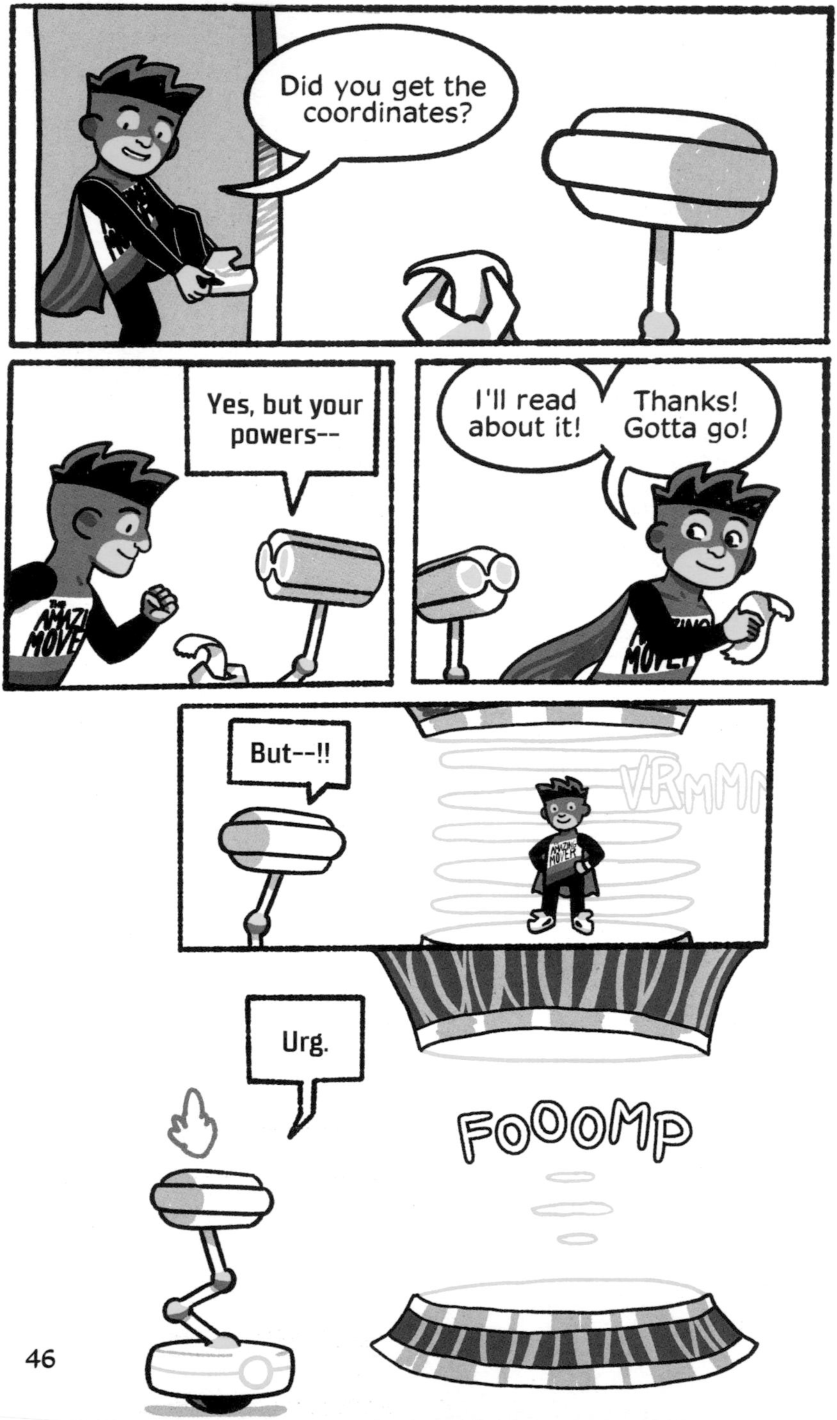
Did you get the coordinates?
Yes, but your powers--
I'll read about it!
Thanks! Gotta go!
But--!!
VRMMM
Urg.
FOOOMP

"Thanks for coming," Tana says, landing her hover-jet. "How'd you get here so fast?"

When I tell her about the teleporter, she actually stops for a second. *"Really?* Even Mr. Valor doesn't have one of those. And he has one of everything."

I don't *have* to tell her it's my mom's, right?

She nods toward the vacuum guy. "That's Mr. Sucko. He's a low-level threat, but it could get messy. He's pulling all the money out of the bank. While the Vrones distract him, I'd like you to use your powers to reverse the airflow of the vacuum and send the money back into the vault."

"Sounds good!" I say.

"If it goes straight back into the bank, I don't have to do as much paperwork—and I hate paperwork." She smiles. "But you have the perfect power for this: moving things!"

The perfect power. A tiny worry twangs in the back of my brain.

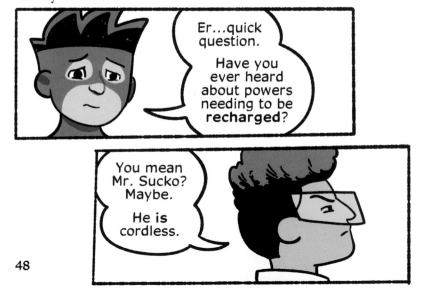

Er...quick question.

Have you ever heard about powers needing to be **recharged**?

You mean Mr. Sucko? Maybe.

He is cordless.

Unfortunately, I don't get to ask any follow-up questions because apparently, it's go time.

"You take the left flank," Tana says.

As I head to the alley, I wonder when Vin Valor will get here. I want him to see me in action! I want him to see my costume! I want him to see that I would be a *great* sidekick.

I guess that can wait, though. For now, I find a spot next to a dumpster. It doesn't smell terrific, but it'll do. The Vrones are starting to swoop, and I can tell things are really heating up.

I've got one eye on Tana, and she gives me the signal. The Vrones begin moving in to distract Mr. Sucko. I lift my arms. Nothing happens. Well, *almost* nothing.

"I'm Mr. Meatballs," the cat says. "What brings you to Chez Alley? That's not the official name, that's just what I call it. This dumpster right here has the best day-old fish anywhere in town."

"Er . . . that must be . . . yum for you . . ." I have no idea how to talk to a talking cat.

The cat seems to realize that, too. It yawns at me.

I forge ahead, answering the question. "I'm using my powers of telekinesis to save the day."

The cat narrows its eyes. "But . . . are you?"

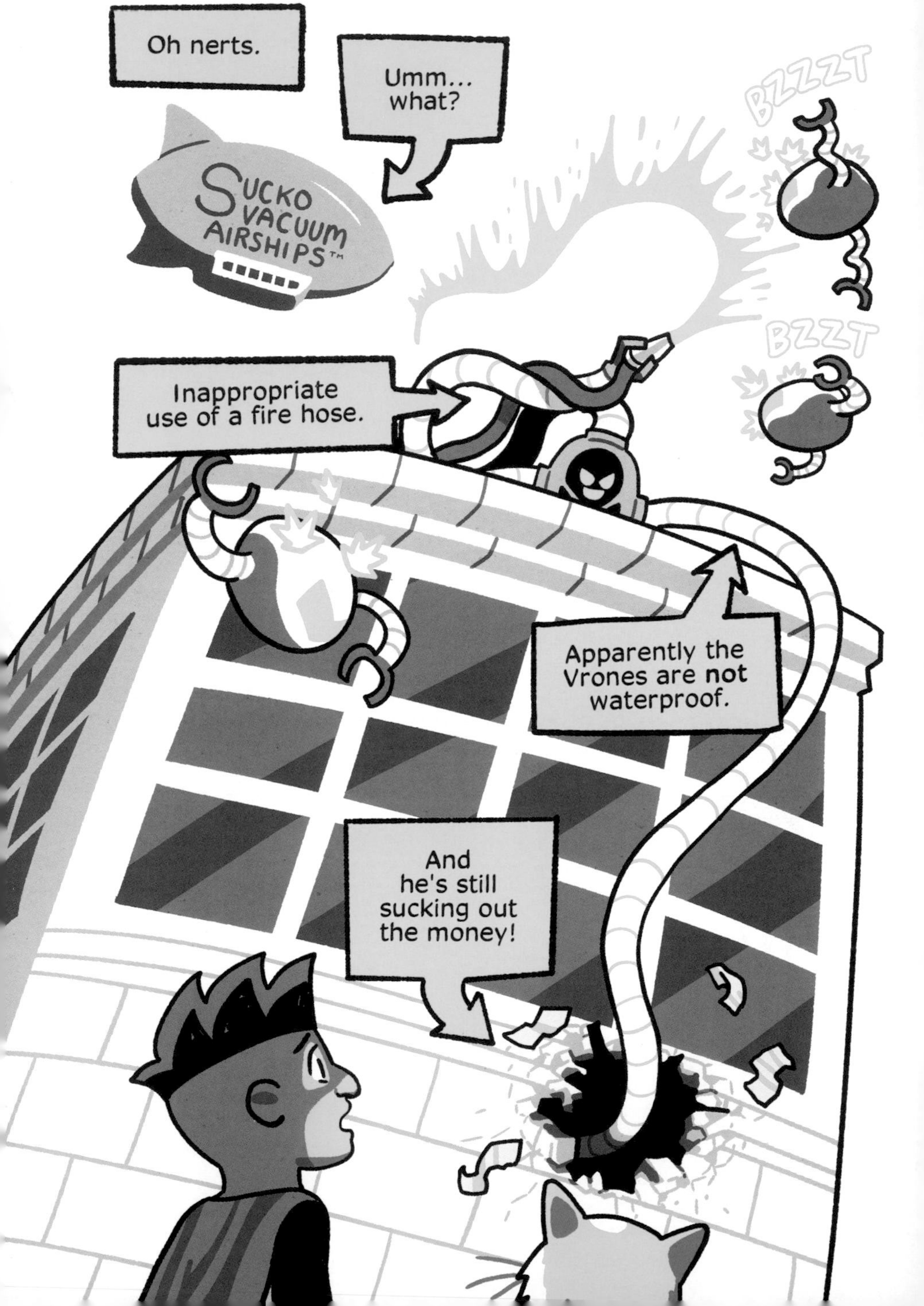
Oh nerts.
Umm... what?
SUCKO VACUUM AIRSHIPS™
BZZZT
BZZT
Inappropriate use of a fire hose.
Apparently the Vrones are **not** waterproof.
And he's still sucking out the money!

"Stop him!" Tana yells from across the way.

"On it!" I yell back. It's not true, though. I'm *not* on it. I'm *trying* to make the money go back into the bank, but it's not working. *At all.*

The glitch again!

Maybe I need to be closer? New plan: I gotta get onto that roof.

The next time one of Mr. Sucko's nozzles swings past me, I grab it . . .

and instantly realize I've made a terrible mistake.

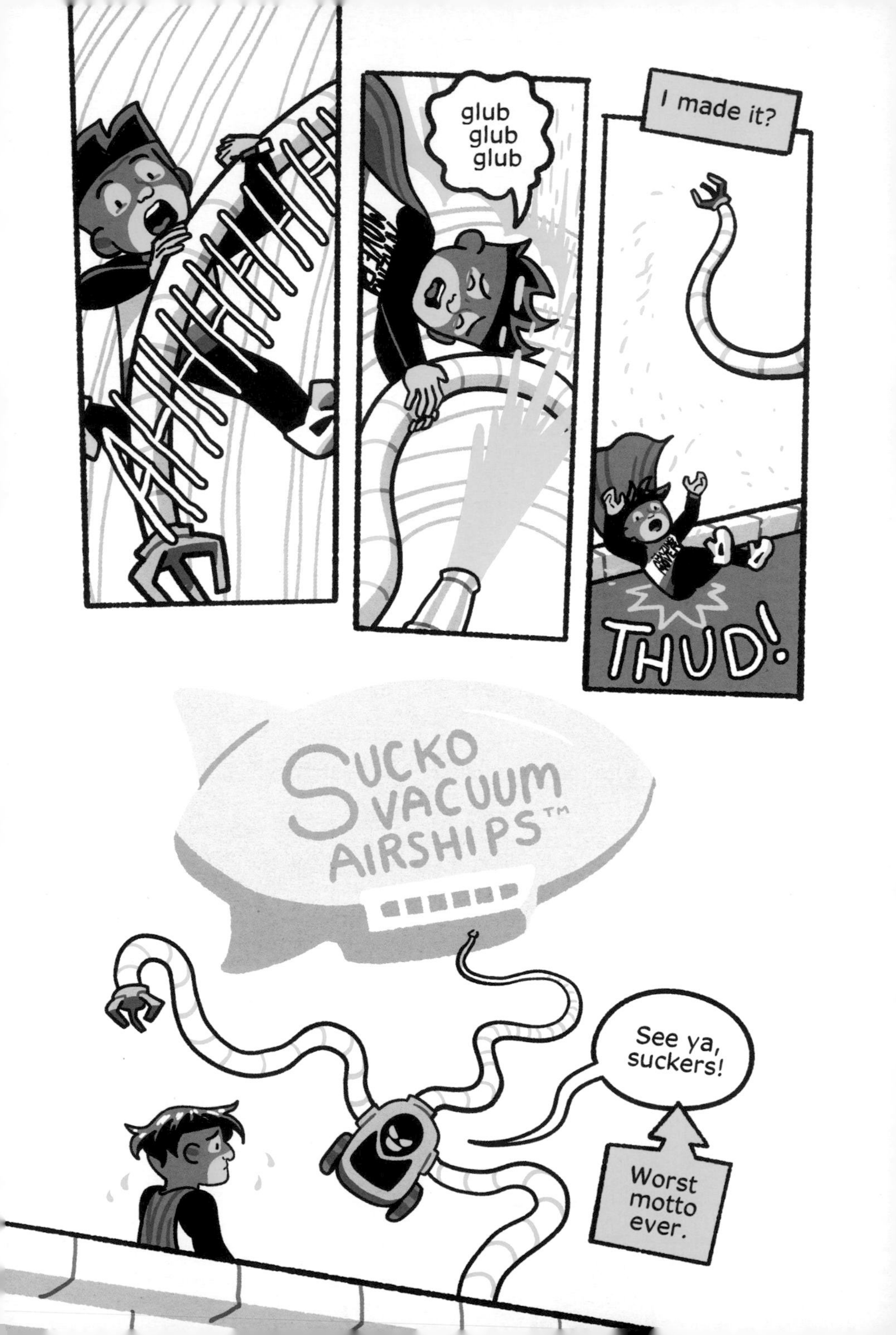
AHHHHHHHH
glub glub glub
MOVERS
I made it?
AMAZING MOVERS
THUD!
SUCKO VACUUM AIRSHIPS™
See ya, suckers!
Worst motto ever.

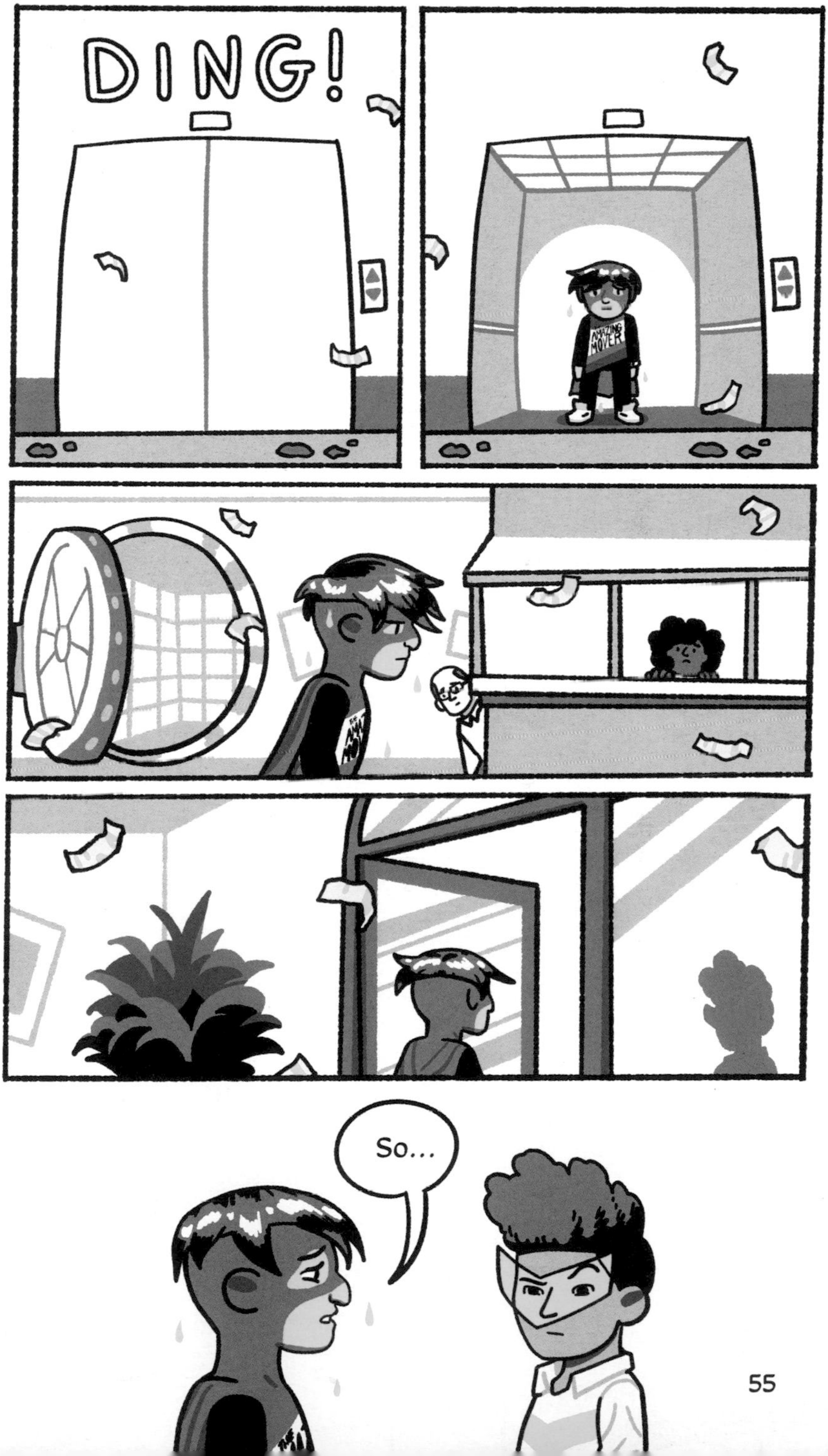
DING!
AMAZING MOVER
So...

It might be because I'm totally soaked. Or because I feel terrible about Mr. Sucko getting away. Or because I'm starting to worry that Mom won't actually be very impressed by all my superheroing.

But maybe it's because I'm feeling all of those things and it's kind of a lot at once, and I just want a friend for a second.

The whole story tumbles out of me. "It's all my fault. I didn't want it to be true, but ever since I woke up, something's been wonky with my powers. They weren't working and I got them checked out right before I came, and they seemed fine, but then when I tried to use them to stop Mr. Sucko, nothing happened. I thought I was okay. I'm sorry."

Maybe Vin Valor doesn't have to know?

Tana frowns at me for a second, then types into her wrist thingy. "Unfortunately, you're still more effective than all of my classmates combined." She looks up. "Don't spread that around."

I honestly can't tell if that's a compliment.

"That vacuum guy totally got away with the money," says a voice from below.

It's the cat.

Of course. And *he* thinks I did a bad job, too.

"Tell me about it," I say glumly. "I just wasn't expecting that getaway airship."

"Nobody was! See, I was watching from the alley," the cat continues, licking a paw. "I'm opposed to vacuum cleaners as it is, but bank-robbing vacuums? I shudder to think of it. And there you were, holding on to one of its arms! Valiant effort, young man."

Maybe I don't mind the cat after all.

"Thanks," I say, hoping Tana might also feel like it was a valiant effort. I glance over at her, but she's looking at me funny.

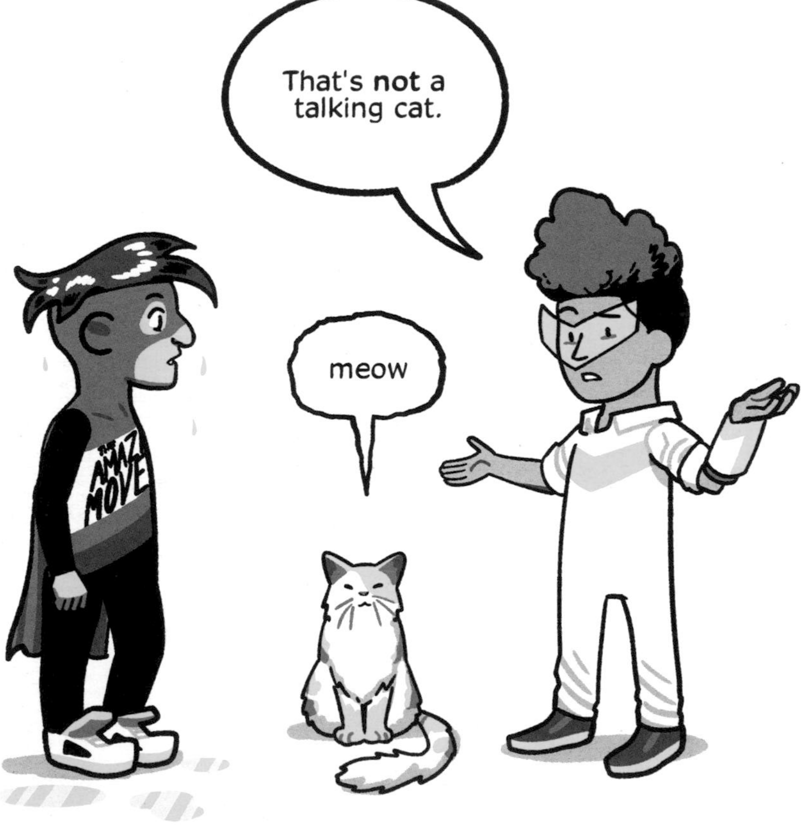
That's **not** a talking cat.
meow

"You're not speaking English?" I ask the cat.

"No," the cat says disdainfully. "I don't speak English. You're speaking Cat."

You've got to be kidding. *Have I been meowing this whole time?* That would be embarrassing, even on a day that has already been nonstop embarrassing on account of my telekinesis not working.

My telekinesis.

Suddenly, I remember the printout, the one from Al. I dig through my pockets furiously, and when I find it, I realize I didn't listen closely enough to Al. *You still have powers,* Al said.

Technically, that was true.

"Here, let me fix it." She leans in with a marker and, before I can stop her, draws right on my Amazing Mover costume. After a second, she steps back and says, "Ta-da!"

"You're disappointed?" Tana asks. "Because your new cat power isn't as flashy as telekinesis?"

"Maybe."

"And maybe because there aren't that many evil cat networks to infiltrate," she says.

I perk up. "Wait, do those actually exist?"

"Er . . . no," she says.

Darn.

"But maybe there will be one day," she says hopefully.

It doesn't seem like Tana has much experience comforting people, but I appreciate the effort.

I look around, realizing that I still haven't heard any jet packs. "Is Vin Valor coming?"

"He's working," Tana says with a shrug. "Something top secret happening in his research lab." She crosses the sidewalk to poke at one of the drenched Vrones.

Sigh. It's probably for the best. If there's any chance of me becoming a sidekick, today would not have been very convincing. Then again, if my only power is speaking Cat, I'm not sure Vin Valor will want me anyway. I feel something push against my leg and look down to see Mr. Meatballs.

"You know," he says, "if you're just standing there, maybe you could give me a little scratch behind the ears?"

I bend down to scratch him, but as I do, I have an idea. A great idea.

"Mr. Meatballs, did you ever watch that movie where the dogs bark to each other across their backyards and send out the warning about the puppies who got stolen—"

I do not watch movies about dogs.

"Oh," I say. "Of course. Sorry."

Mr. Meatballs sniffs like he halfway accepts my apology.

"I was just wondering," I say carefully. "I know there isn't an evil cat network. But is there maybe a *non-evil* cat network? And maybe you could ask around and see if any cats saw where Mr. Sucko went? That would be super helpful."

Mr. Meatballs frowns. "It'll be tricky with him up in the air like that," he says. "Also with this being such good nap weather. But I'll give it a shot."

And then he's gone. Maybe this *will* work!

"Tana," I call out. "Do you want help cleaning up again?" I don't mention that it's mostly my fault that everything went wrong, so I should probably do *all* the cleanup.

The sidewalk is a mess, and I've just finished filling up my third trash can when Mr. Meatballs returns.

I've got good news and bad news.

"The bad news," Mr. Meatballs says, "is that nobody was awake to see where he went."

It's hard not to be disappointed, but maybe I just need to work on the idea a little more. Get to know the cat network myself. Convince them not to take so many naps?

I look over to see that Tana and the Vrones are all ready to go. Even with the cat network idea, I have to admit I'm nervous that this is it. Will I ever see Tana again? Or come to Vin Valor's aid?

I dig into my muffin and tell Al all about it. About how gigantically I failed. About how Tana thinks I'm just a big cat joke. About how Vin Valor is probably majorly disappointed over the report explaining that I have a totally, completely, absolutely useless power now.

"Not *completely* useless," says a voice from near the ground.

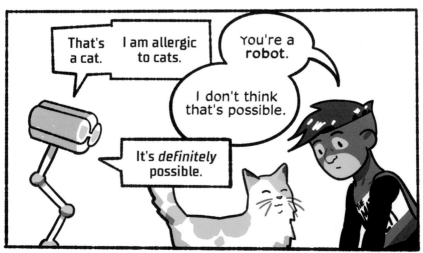

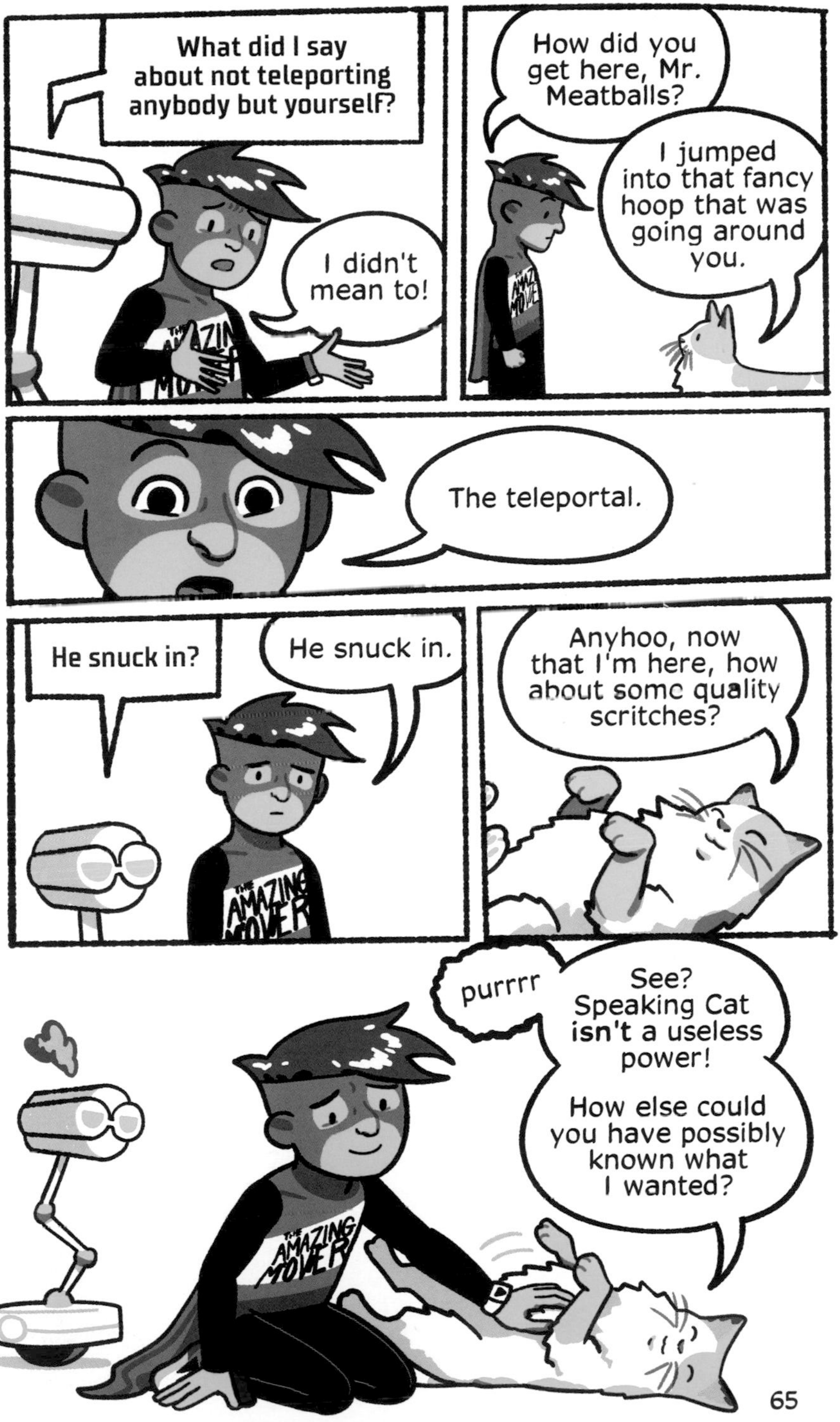
What did I say about not teleporting anybody but yourself?
I didn't mean to!
How did you get here, Mr. Meatballs?
I jumped into that fancy hoop that was going around you.
The teleportal.
He snuck in?
He snuck in.
Anyhoo, now that I'm here, how about some quality scritches?
purrrr
See? Speaking Cat **isn't** a useless power!
How else could you have possibly known what I wanted?

I convince Al to let Mr. Meatballs stay for the night, and after the cat curls up and falls asleep, I try to get myself sorted.

I come up with a brand-new design.

It's purrfect.

I hand the design over to Al.

Then I record everything in my journal, even the terrible, embarrassing details, like any good super-hero—or any good scientist—would do.

I can't help wondering what Mom will think about me forming a non-evil cat network based out of the house. I mean, she likes *cats*. Just not really superhero comics.

I'll just have to find the right way to tell her. And maybe I'll change her mind about superheroes!

Knock, knock.

Who's there?

Orange.

Orange who?

Orange you glad your son is a superhero?

It makes me laugh for a second, until I realize how much I miss the sound of *her* laughing.

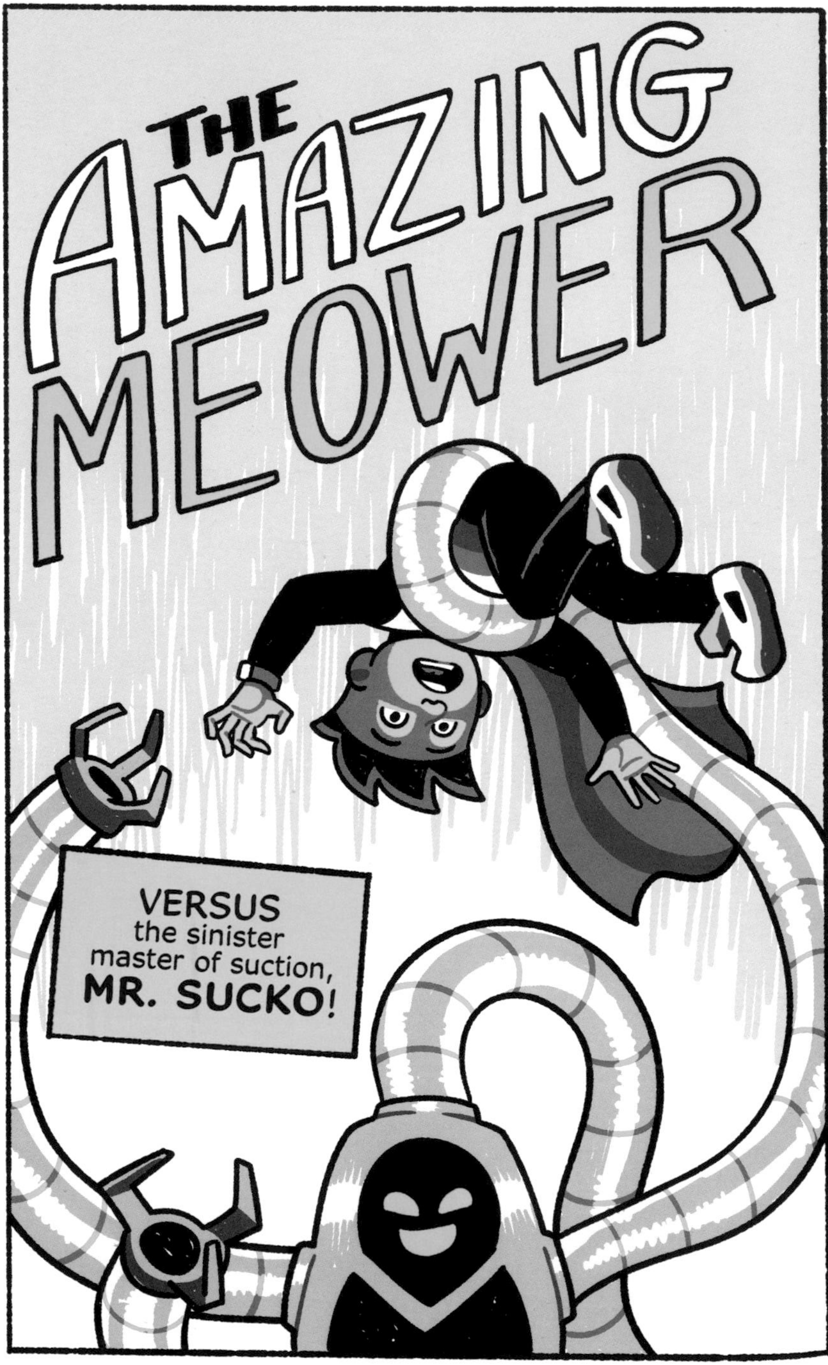
THE AMAZING MEOWER
VERSUS the sinister master of suction, MR. SUCKO!

CHAPTER 3

Dawn breaks and the **Amazing Meower** leaps out of bed!

He and his legion of cats are **unstoppable**!

Even his **mom** thinks it's cool!

Now I just need to figure out how to build a ~~cat army~~ non-evil cat network! I head to the kitchen, accidentally tripping over Mr. Meatballs, who is lying right in the doorway.

I turn around to ask Mr. Meatballs if that was *supposed* to be a joke, when suddenly . . .

EVERYTHING IS GIGANTIC.

Nope. That's not it.

I AM TINY.

This doesn't seem great. "Mr. Meatballs!" I yell. "Help! Get Al!"

Mr. Meatballs is staring at me. He looks very concerned. But he is distinctly *not* going for help.

"Okay," I say, "just to make sure, no joking around, can you definitely NOT understand me right now?"

Mr. Meatballs meows, like, eighteen times in a row. He's saying a lot. And I am for sure not understanding.

Not one single meow.

My stomach sinks. Another superpower, gone.

I need Al.
Time to use my massive charades skills.

Mr. Meatballs has clearly not played a lot of charades in his life. Because . . .

"It's me," I say.

Al looks at me up close. "You shrunk?"

"I shrunk. Scan me?"

"Well . . . now it's official?" Al offers.

That does *not* help. Suddenly, I wish Mom was here. Not so I could show off my new powers or so I could convince her how awesome superheroes are—I just want her to make me feel better.

Because I don't really understand what's happening. Is something wrong with me? I need to stop glitching.

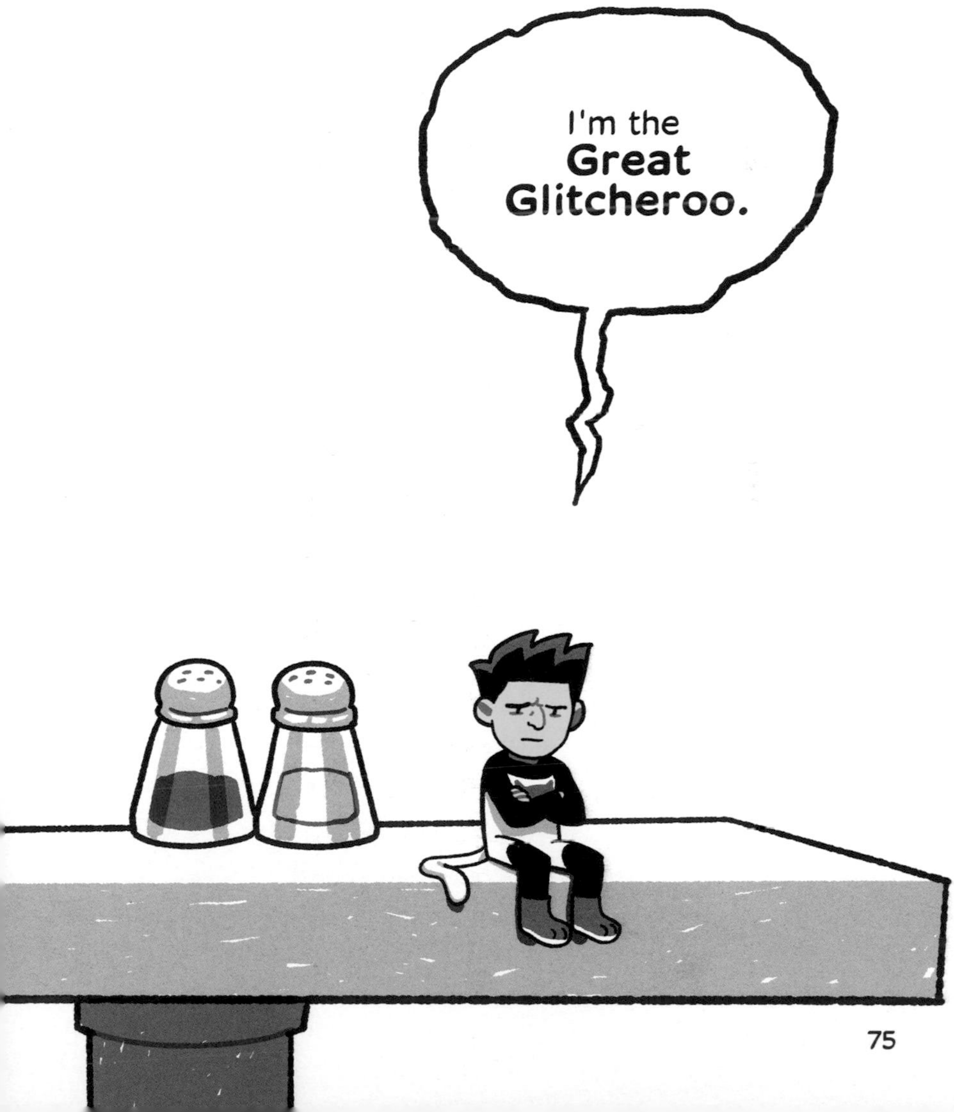
I'm the Great Glitcheroo.

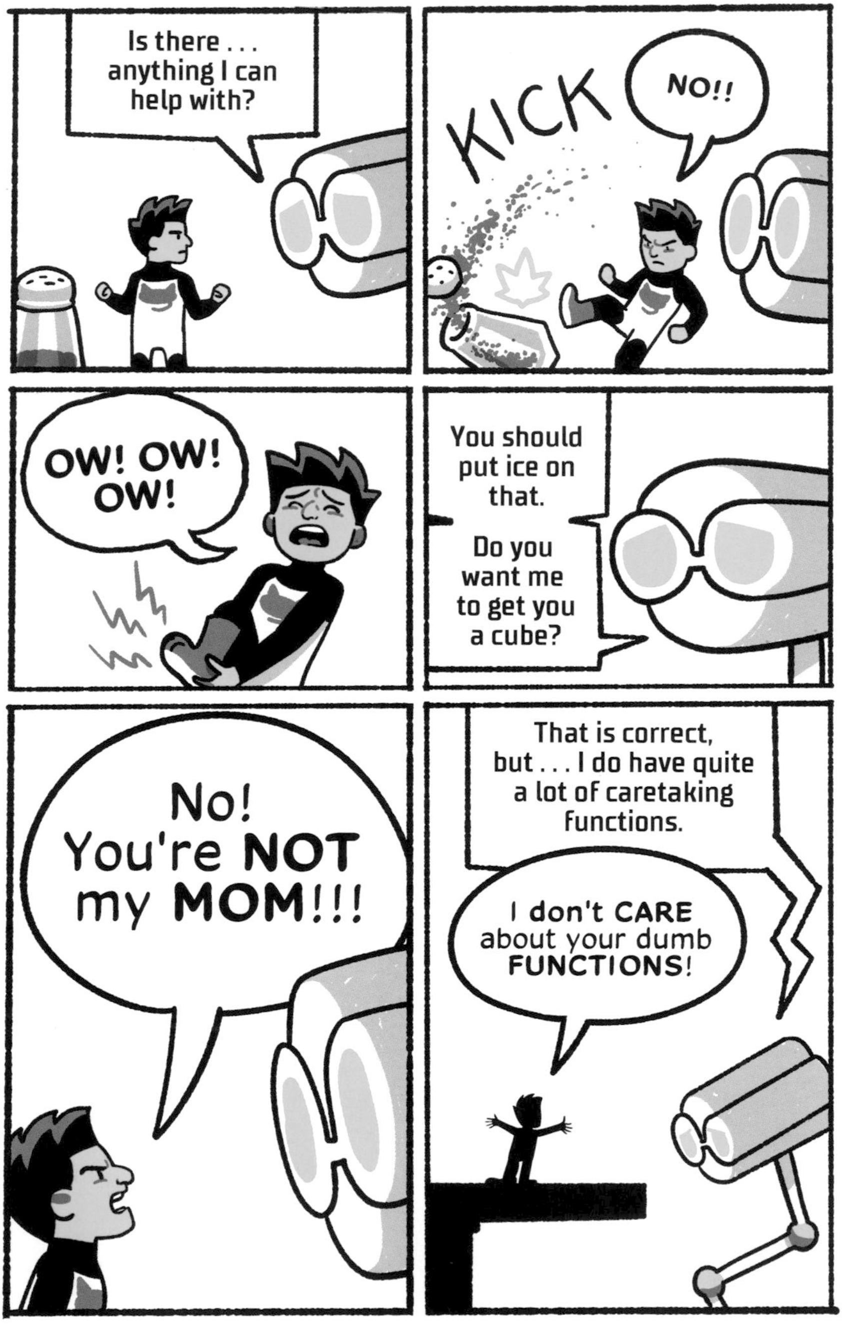
Is there . . .
anything I can
help with?
KICK
NO!!
OW! OW!
OW!
You should
put ice on
that.
Do you
want me
to get you
a cube?
No!
You're **NOT**
my **MOM**!!!
That is correct,
but . . . I do have quite
a lot of caretaking
functions.
I **don't CARE**
about your dumb
FUNCTIONS!

Suddenly, there's a buzzing. From Al. From the hologram phone.

Mom? I think before I can stop myself. But then a hologram of Tana Gregorio appears in the kitchen.

"Hi," she says, typing furiously on the computer. Tana definitely seems like a multitasker.

"Hi, Tana," I say, pulling it together. "Things are a little weird today. I might not be very helpful. You know, in a superhero kind of way."

I'm having a **small** problem.

Tana nods and keeps going like she barely even heard me. "Right. It's fine, there's no current emergency. Except, well . . . so, this morning, I . . . something weird happened. Look, if you get any suspicious communications, you need to tell me right away."

"Oh," I say. "Okay. Sure."

"Thanks!"

"What happened this morni—" I start to ask her, but then realize I'm talking to nobody. She's hung up on me. It's odd, but that's Tana.

Anyway, I have enough problems without having to worry about why Tana's getting suspicious communications.

"Al, would you call Mom again?" I pace across the table as the call goes to voicemail. Again.

Why is she IGNORING me??

"Perhaps we could—" Al begins.

"I don't need your help."

Al rolls back in surprise.

"You don't know where Mom is, do you?"

"Her location is currently unknown," Al says.

"Well, that's the only thing I need! So if you can't tell me that, then what's the point? Mom's gone and I *need* her right now. You wouldn't understand."

"I might—"

"Something is *wrong* with me. What if tomorrow's power is that I turn into a rock and I can't turn myself back? Who's going to take care of me?"

What do you think I'VE been doing?!?!

I start to sputter a response, but the thing is . . . Al's right. Al's totally right.

Nerts.

And as weird as this sounds, it looks like I hurt Al's feelings. I'm not okay with that.

I take a deep breath.

I'm sorry. I was being a jerk.

"What's that?" asks Al. "I couldn't hear you. You're going to have to say it louder. A LOT louder."

I'm pretty sure Al can hear me just fine, but maybe I deserve that. So I say it again, louder this time.

Since we're being all honest and stuff here, I make myself say the thing I really don't want to. "Do you think something might have happened? To Mom?"

"I'm sure she's fine . . ." Al sees the look on my face. "But I will check into it."

"Thanks," I say quietly.

"And right now, I should get back to cleaning the lab."

"Do you want help?"

That's how I end up on cotton ball duty.

I'm a few shelves in when a familiar smell drifts up my nostrils. It's exactly the same as that bubble bath Al gave me a few days ago.

And it's coming from this bottle.

This must be a coincidence, the smell. Right?

"Al?" I call out. Al's a few feet away, sweeping around Mr. Meatballs, who's asleep in the middle of the floor. "You know that rad bubble bath you set up for me a few days ago? What made you do that? Did I smell really bad or something?"

"No," Al says without a break in the sweeping. "I was following protocol."

I stop dusting. "Protocol? For what?"

"I got the encrypted message requiring me to draw that bath for you."

"From Mom," Al says, and my stomach drops into my feet. I'm still tiny, so it's not a very far drop, but it sure does feel like it.

That doesn't make any sense.

And honestly, as weird as all this is, I'm also suddenly, overwhelmingly . . . jealous. Mom's been gone over a week, and she hasn't talked to me at all, but she sent Al a secret message.

I would have liked a secret message.

"It was a short message," Al explains. "*Prepare the radium bath.*"

Instantly, I forget about being jealous.

My skin prickles.

Rad bath, Al had said. But it wasn't a *cool* bath. A *neato* bath. An *awesome* bath.

It was a RADIUM bath!

"Al, why would Mom want you to give me a radium bath?" I ask, stunned. "Isn't radium *radioactive?*"

"I have been programmed not to ask her those sorts of questions," Al explains.

"Well, *I* haven't," I say. "And now I have a LOT of questions."

Did Mom know that I was going to get powers? Did she try to stop it?

And why was the message encrypted?

It's all got to mean something. I just have to figure out what.

I go back to dusting, but it's half-hearted. My mind is buzzing with questions. And since Mom's not here to answer them, I'm going to have to solve them myself.

That's what I'm thinking when I hear an eardrum-bursting *MREOW* from behind me.

"Al, did you *sweep* him?" I ask as I turn around.

"I did not," Al says indignantly.

"Well, yes—"

"*You expect me to feed him?*" Al asks incredulously.

"MREOW," cries Mr. Meatballs.

"I am afraid"—Al's voice gets low—"we have a cat problem."

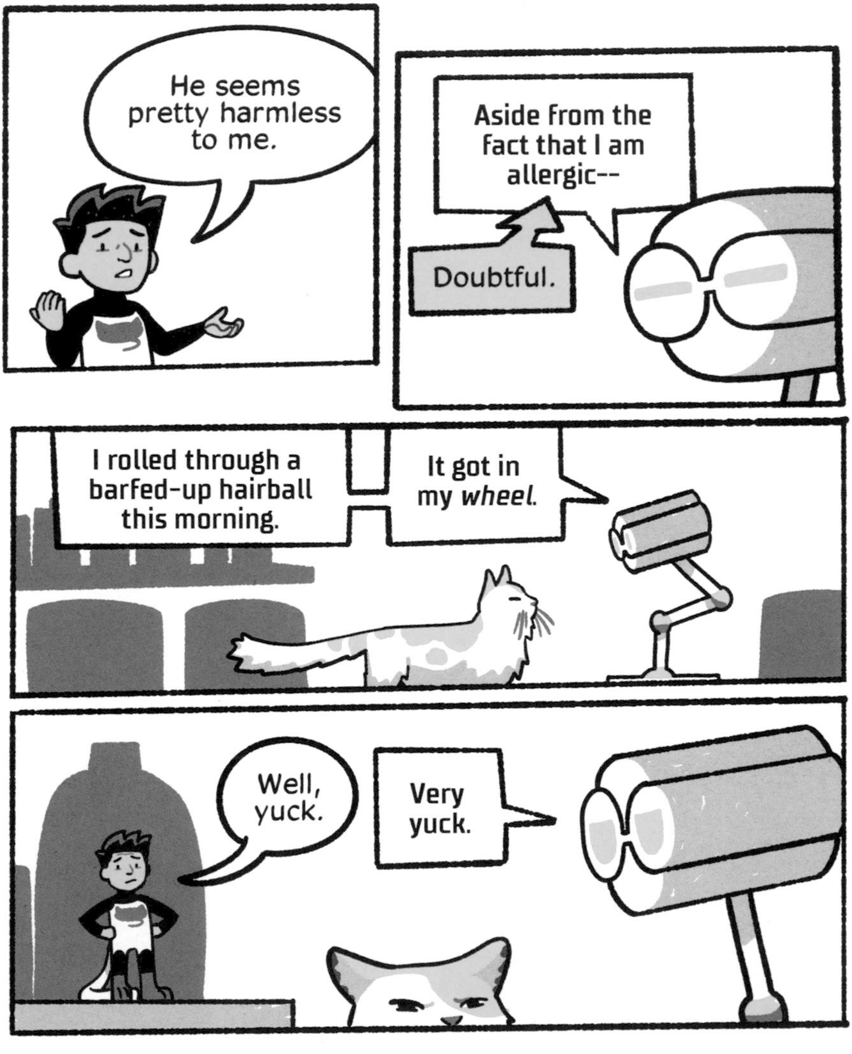
He seems pretty harmless to me.
Aside from the fact that I am allergic--
Doubtful.
I rolled through a barfed-up hairball this morning.
It got in my *wheel*.
Well, yuck.
Very yuck.

I'm not exactly excited about the hairball situation. And I did think Mr. Meatballs was only going to hang around for one night.

On the other hand, I'm not going to dump him outside if he doesn't want to be there. "I'll figure it out," I say. "For now, maybe you could just give him some tuna?"

"I'm done with the bottles," I call out. "Anything else you want me to work on?"

Al points to the lab sink. "There's a clog in the drain—I was going to do it, but one of my very few faults is that I hate gross stuff."

I peer over the edge of the drain and realize that the simplest way to do this will be to climb down into it.

Gross, indeed.

Once I've lowered myself to the clog, I start untangling it, when suddenly my hand hits something hard. And metal.

That's strange.

I peel away layer after disgusting layer of slimy, grimy gunk until I get down to the inside of the whole thing.

It's a key. There's a key stuck in the drain.

I climb out of the drain and haul the key up after me.

After a few embarrassing minutes that I won't tell you about, I manage to get normal-sized again. I dry off, ignore how bad I smell, and examine the key.

Why did Mom throw a key down a drain? And what door does it open?

Al reappears (along with a very satisfied Mr. Meatballs) and blinks at me. "Normal-sized again, are we?"

"We are," I say, but before I can ask about the key, Al hands me a printout.

"You just got an email," Al explains. "It's from Suxjr at AOL dot com."

"I don't know anybody named Suxjr."

"Well, whoever that is sent you an email."

"Are you reading my email?" I ask.

"No," Al says, frowning. "Only sometimes."

TO: VinValorSuperFan@powerstation.com
FROM: Suxjr@aol.com

Leave my dad alone. Or else.

It's hard to explain the weird feeling in my gut, but I try anyway. "I know what I'm *supposed* to do—but something inside me says that I shouldn't tell Tana about this message."

Al frowns. "Are you sure about that?"

"Of course I'm not sure!" I explode, suddenly angrier and sadder than I realized. "I'm not sure of *any*thing! I don't know what dumb superpower I'm going to have tomorrow! There's all these secrets, and I don't know who sent that message or why, I don't know why I have a weird feeling about telling Tana, I don't know where Mom is or why she sent you that encrypted message about the bath! I don't even know who I can trust anymore!"

"You can trust me," Al says.

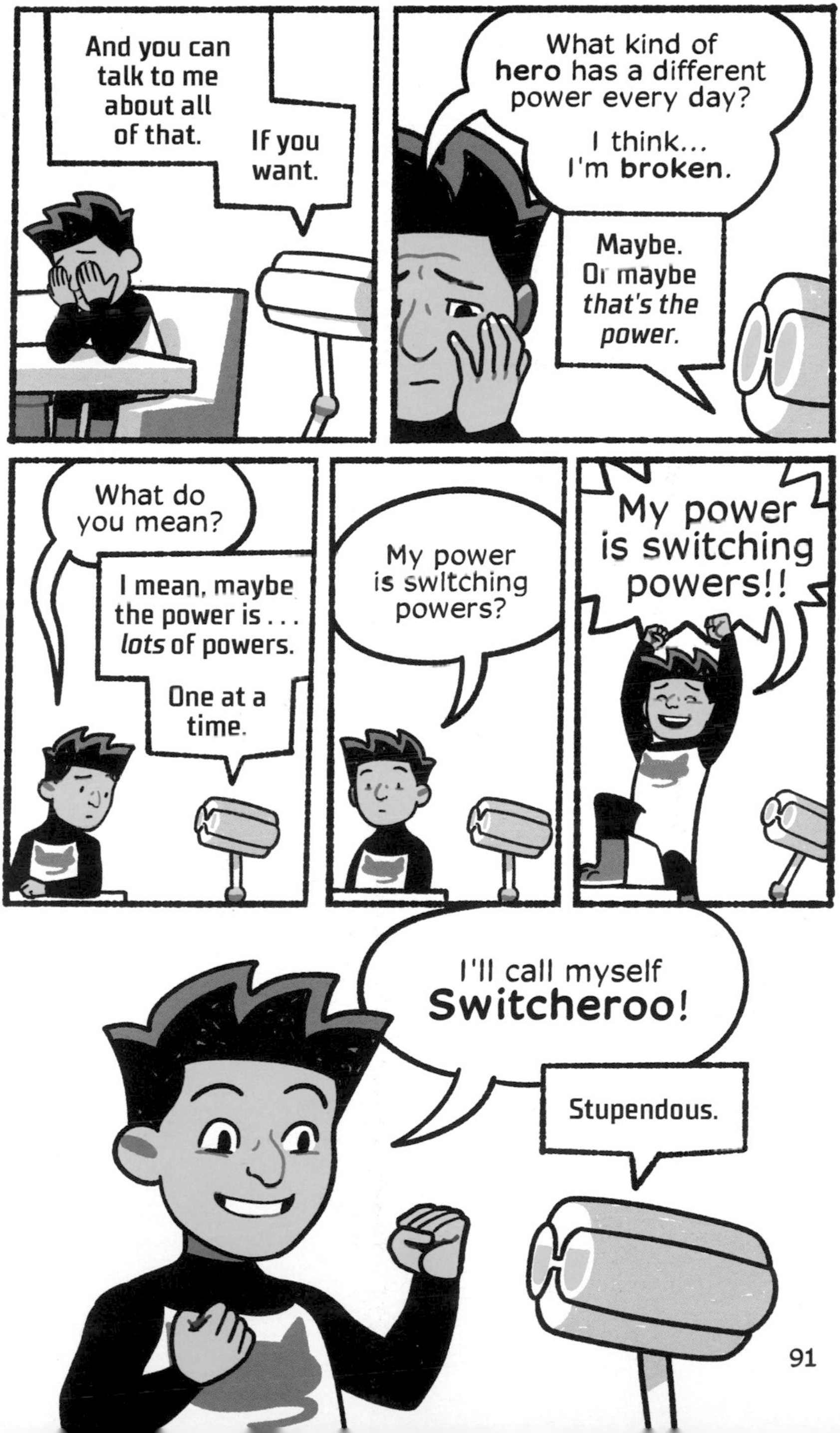
And you can talk to me about all of that.
If you want.
What kind of **hero** has a different power every day?
I think... I'm **broken**.
Maybe. Or maybe *that's the power.*
What do you mean?
I mean, maybe the power is . . . *lots* of powers.
One at a time.
My power is switching powers?
My power is switching powers!!
I'll call myself **Switcheroo**!
Stupendous.

"And every day that I get a new power," I say slowly, figuring it out in my mind, "is a new way to help people. It's a new way to fight villains."

"Exactly," says Al. "You'll have to be creative . . ."

"But I'll make the most out of whatever power I have!"

"I think that's a very smart plan," says Al with a robot-y smile.

"I had some help," I say, smiling back. "*Speaking* of help . . . I'll need a new costume."

"With pizzazz?" asks Al.

"With pizzazz."

Al and I work late into the night, cutting material and sewing it together. It's the most fun I've had in a long time.

To be honest, it was scary at first.

Realizing that I couldn't control my own superhero destiny from day to day.

But now, I think I've changed my mind about it. It's not scary—it's *exciting* knowing I'll have a different power tomorrow, and I don't have a clue what it'll be. Maybe I'll be able to work with Vin Valor and fight more villains. Maybe I'll be able to save people who are in trouble. I know I'll figure it out. I mean, with Al's help, of course. And maybe Mr. Meatballs, even.

And when Mom *does* come home, she'll be super proud.

Of me, the Stupendous Switcheroo.

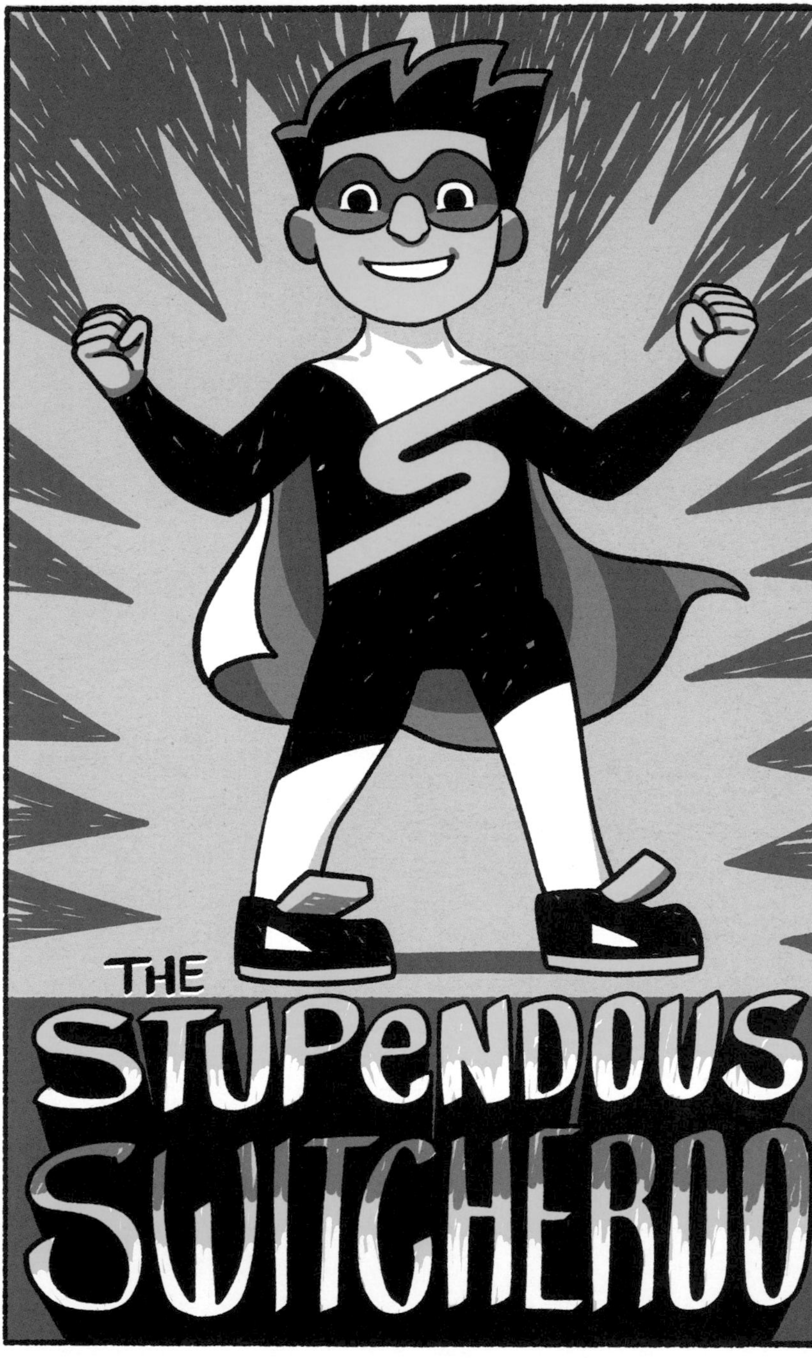
THE
STUPENDOUS
SWITCHEROO

CHAPTER 4

I get out of bed and put on my Stupendous Switcheroo costume and shoes and mask and I am SO ready for today and I think my new power might be the power of positive thinking because I'm already positive I'm going to solve ALL the mysteries, starting with The Mystery of the Mysterious Email—yesterday I was worried about it, but today, I don't know, it seems obvious that I should just write back, so I pull up the email from Suxjr and hit reply!

TO: Suxjr@aol.com

FROM: VinValorSuperFan@powerstation.com

Dear Suxjr,

I don't know what you're talking about. How did you get this email? Maybe you have the wrong person. I'm almost definitely the wrong person. Do *you* think you have the wrong person? I don't know what's going on with your dad, but I hope he's okay.

Sincerely,
The Stupendous Switcheroo

SEND!

I give myself a high five and then get ready to work on the next mystery: The Mystery of the Weird Key That Was Stuck in the Drain!

I bet I know exactly who can help me with that (Al!) so I go into the kitchen to find Al and oooh I smell toast and some other really delicious stuff so I eat my entire breakfast before Al stops me right as I'm washing off my plate—

But aside from the eggs . . . this is perfect!

"A day with super speed is *exactly* what I need," I tell Al. "I have SO much to do! I'll start by going through the entire house and figuring out what this key opens and then after that—"

"Meow." Mr. Meatballs appears out of nowhere, looking impatiently at Al.

I start again. "After that, I'll—"

"MEOW," Mr. Meatballs interrupts again.

Hmm. "Did you ever feed him?" I ask Al.

"Of *course* I did. This is . . . the other thing," Al says meaningfully.

I don't get it.

"The *other* thing," Al repeats.

I frown.

"I refuse to have a litterbox in here," Al finally says, exasperated.

I am a sophisticated, state-of-the-art *robot*.

Not a pooper-scooper.

No litterbox seems... risky.

"Mr. Meatballs and I have worked out a system," Al explains. "I gave him a collar that connects to the teleporter's signal. I can teleport him away when he needs to go—"

"*MEOW,*" Mr. Meatballs says urgently.

Teleport him! Of course! I pick up Mr. Meatballs, dash to the teleporter with my super speed, and quickly teleport the cat outside.

"What are you *doing*?" Al zips after me.

"Saving the day!" I holler. "This cat needs to GO!"

Al nudges me aside, pushes a few buttons, and Mr. Meatballs teleports back immediately.

Hm. Must've been raining.

"The cat and I have a *system*. And *you* are still learning how to use the teleporter!" Al frowns at me and pushes more buttons, and the grumpy cat disappears again.

"And now we *wait*," Al says. "When he's ready, he meows into the mic on his collar, and that triggers a green light so I know to bring him back. And *no,* you can't hurry the process. Trust me, I've tried. It was . . . not pretty."

"Okay," I say. "But I can't wait around FOREVER, I've got MYSTERIES to solve!"

"You are going to be *incorrigible* today," Al says, looking at me sideways. "Aren't you?"

"Is that related to oatmeal?" I ask. "Like porridge? Are you calling me inedible?" To be honest, my mind is going so fast I'm having a hard time keeping up. So instead of trying to understand, I just say, "I'll be right back!"

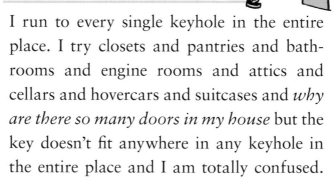

I run to every single keyhole in the entire place. I try closets and pantries and bathrooms and engine rooms and attics and cellars and hovercars and suitcases and *why are there so many doors in my house* but the key doesn't fit anywhere in any keyhole in the entire place and I am totally confused.

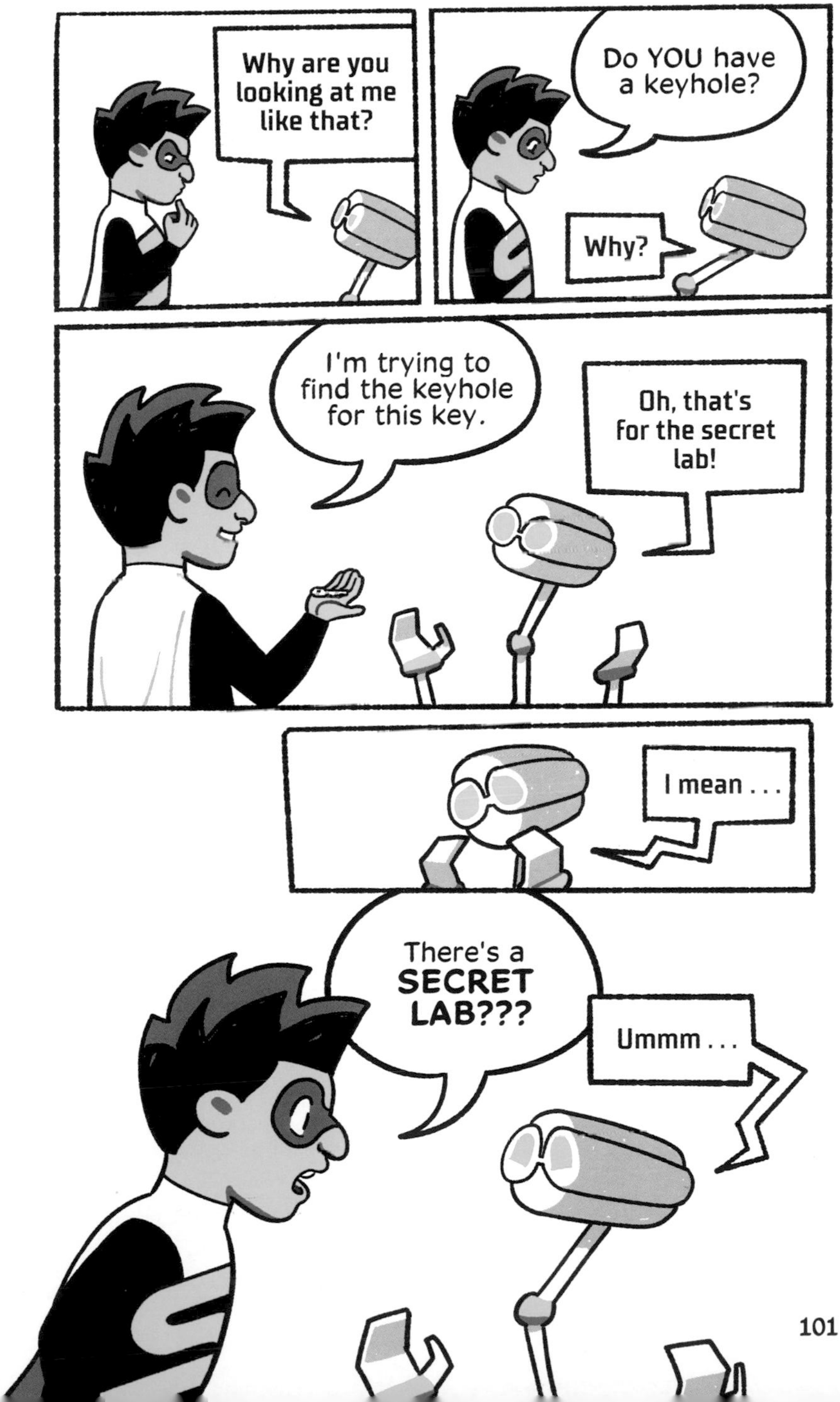
Why are you looking at me like that?
Do YOU have a keyhole?
Why?
I'm trying to find the keyhole for this key.
Oh, that's for the secret lab!
I mean . . .
There's a SECRET LAB???
Ummm . . .

Obviously, I have to see the secret lab.

ASAP.

Al grumbles a little about having to wait for Mr. Meatballs, but a second later, we're in my mom's NON-secret lab, standing next to the giant painting of the periodic table she has hanging on the wall.

Every single element, listed in its place, from hydrogen to oganesson. I've seen the painting a million times, and I'm totally unprepared for what happens next.

Al goes to the bottom left corner and lifts up the panel that says *radium*.

There's a keyhole underneath.

I turn the key.

The periodic table shudders and begins to slide open, separating down the middle and revealing a door right in front of where I'm standing.

I can hardly breathe.

I push the door open.

"It's just, you know, Mr. Meatballs," Al says nervously. "I need to be watching for that green light? So . . . just . . . please don't touch anything?"

I don't answer and Al rolls off anyway.

I step into the secret lab, and for the first time all day, I'm moving slowly. It makes me feel like the ground is wobbly, discovering that Mom kept all these secrets from me.

Maybe I don't know her as well as I think I do.

This room looks exactly like you'd imagine a secret lab would look. There's a table in the middle of the room, stacked high with papers and books. One wall has a huge whiteboard, covered with Mom's scrawling handwriting. File cabinets line the rest of the walls.

What was she doing in here?

I step over to the closest file cabinet, and the label catches my eye.

Wait. Like, *my* Mr. Sucko? How many Mr. Suckos can there be?

Next to that, there's one labeled *Lou Ooze.*

Why does Mom have files on these villains? I reach out to open the drawer . . .

And Al hollers my name, making me jump about a foot! I zoom through the house and arrive to see a hologram of Tana.

"Hi, Tana— " I start to say.

Al stops me. "It's a video message."

Which makes sense, since she's still talking. ". . . there aren't any cats here today, but I could really just use any help I can get . . ." She begins running, and I realize she's already dealing with a villain! "I'm at the Great Spiral Monument. The Shadow's Shadow is threatening the communications tower on top— Oh no! Just come if you can!"

Hold up. THE SHADOW'S SHADOW????

I've read ALL about him!

Nobody knows what the Shadow's Shadow is *exactly*—an actual shadow from some person somewhere? Dark matter, like from space? A ghost?

He's EXTREMELY mysterious.

But this much is definite: nobody has ever captured him. Vin Valor has stopped plenty of his evil schemes . . . but he always gets away. Always.

So, yeah, I want to know what's in my mom's files—but it can wait. I'm going to try out my super speed against the Shadow's Shadow!!!

It isn't easy to convince Al, but *finally* I'm in the teleporter (after promising to be very careful).

Here's the amazing thing: because of the Vin Valor comics, *I totally know how to defeat the Shadow's Shadow!* (And you better bet I'm going to tell Mom that reading all those comics actually WAS a worthwhile investment of my time!)

"I got this!" I holler, and then, thanks to my super speed, I run to the closest used-car lot and back to the Great Spiral before Tana finishes asking me what I'm doing.

Clearly, Tana has never read *Vin Valor,* Issue 27, "Valor Against the Shadows," because there's a very simple way to defeat the Shadow's Shadow, who is, after all, a very big shadow.

All you need is more light.

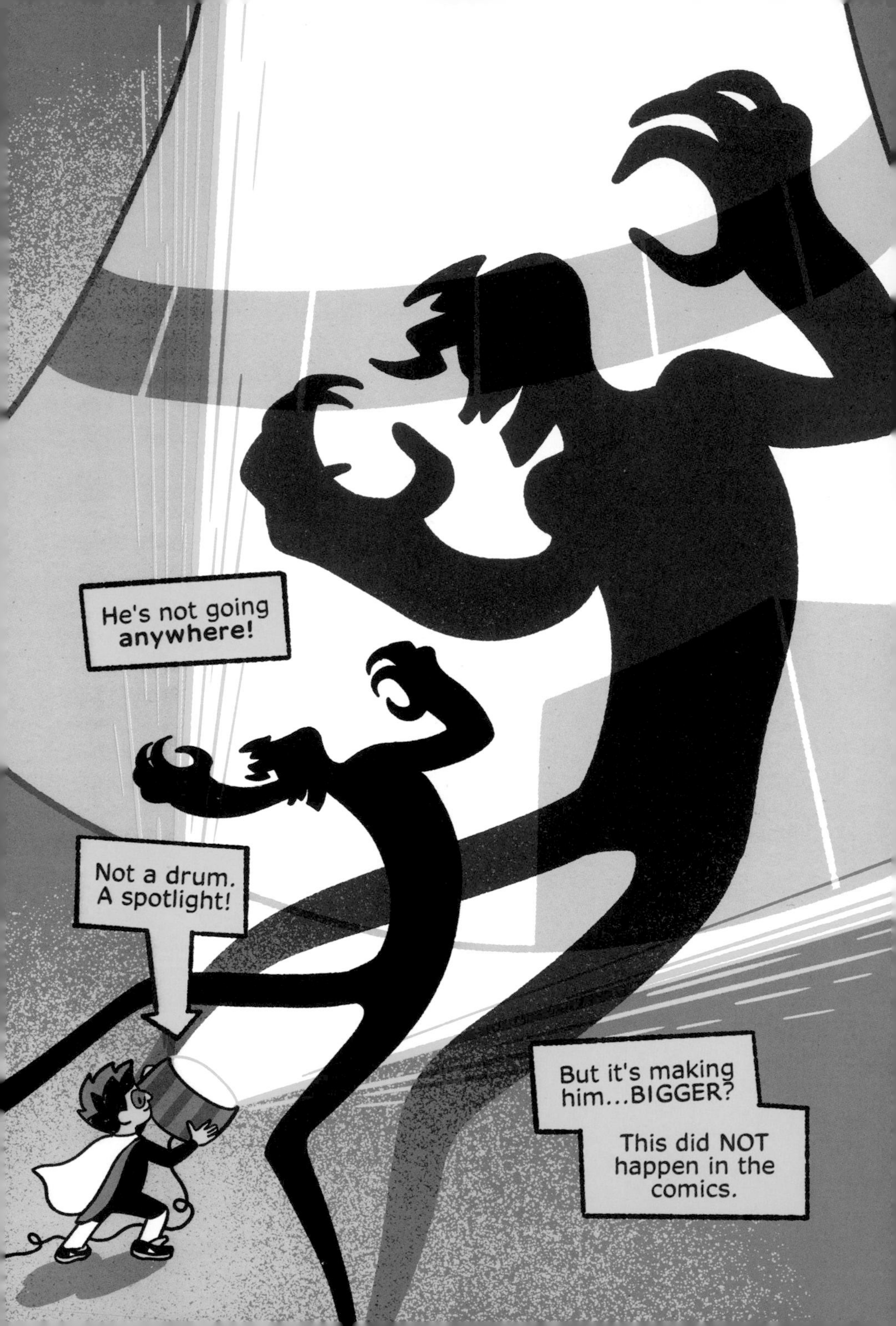
He's not going **anywhere!**
Not a drum. A spotlight!
But it's making him...BIGGER?
This did NOT happen in the comics.

"So . . ." Tana stares as the bigger, stronger super-villain starts climbing up the monument. "WHY did you make him more powerful?"

"I didn't mean to!" I say. "I was doing what Vin Valor does in Issue 27—"

"'Valor Against the Shadows'?" Tana finishes my sentence for me. "That's a comic book! It didn't really happen! It was a *story*!"

Well, I'm not telling Mom about this now.

"You can't just run around and do stuff without telling me!" she says, throwing her hands in the air. "Now he's *definitely* going to be able to tear down the VTech communicator on top!"

Noooooooooo!

I sneak a look at Tana. She seems really worried—and I realize with a start that this might get her in trouble with Vin Valor. Even though it's my fault. I *really* don't want to mess things up for her—not again. First the whole Mr. Sucko disaster, and now this . . .

Wait a minute—Mr. Sucko! The file cabinet I was about to open before I left! The files on Mr. Sucko and Lou Ooze . . . maybe my mom had one for the Shadow's Shadow? Is that possible?

"I'll be right back!" I yell to Tana as I teleport home, zip past Al, zoom through the house, and screech to a halt in the secret lab.

It takes me about one second to find what I'm looking for.

HOW TO DEFEAT:
Blue luxolyte exposure to dematerialize.

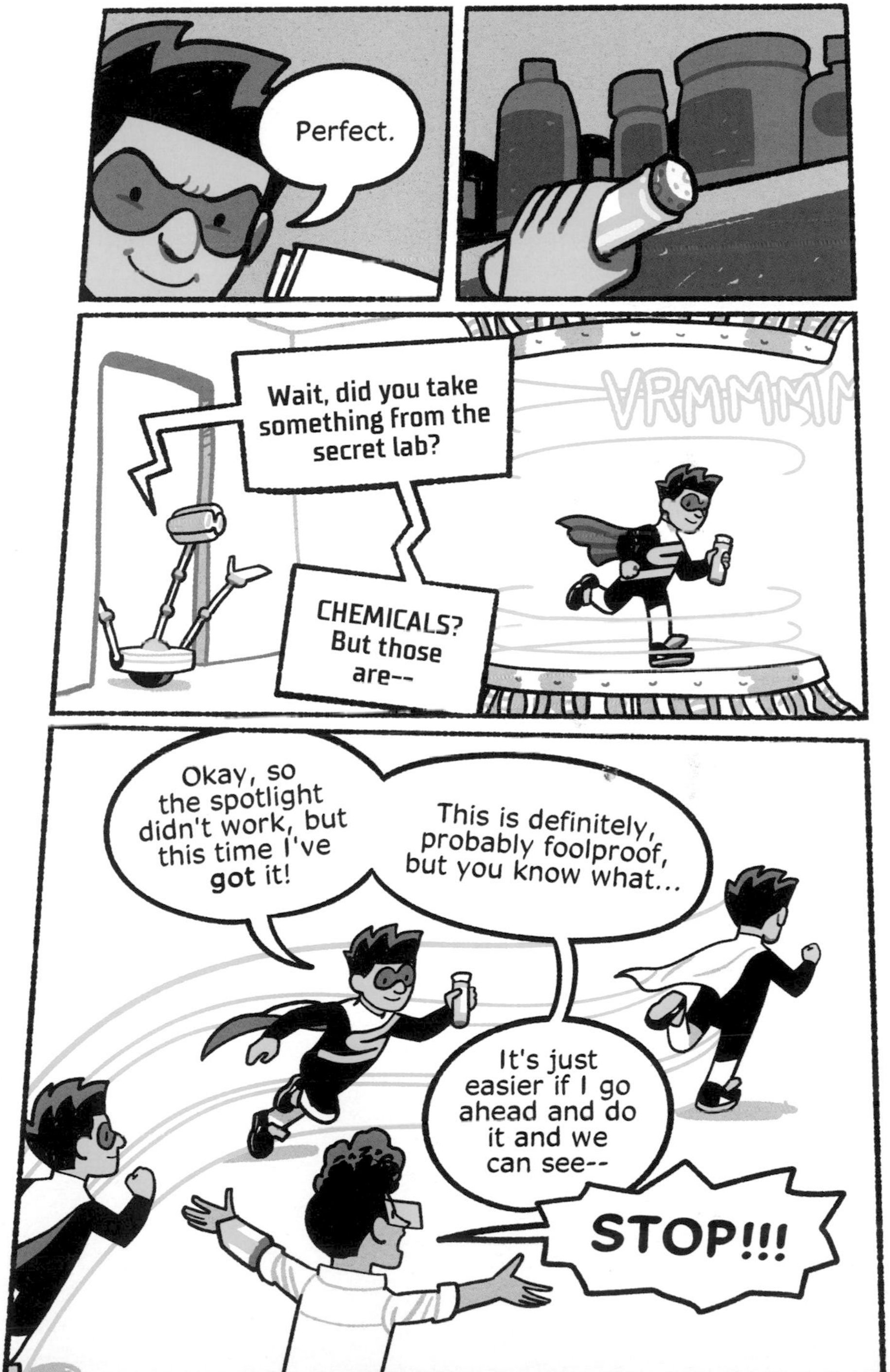

Perfect.
Wait, did you take something from the secret lab?
VRMMMM
CHEMICALS? But those are--
Okay, so the spotlight didn't work, but this time I've **got** it!
This is definitely, probably foolproof, but you know what...
It's just easier if I go ahead and do it and we can see--
STOP!!!

"What's wrong?" I ask.

"You!" Tana says, pointing right at me. "You're out of control!"

"But I have the real solution this time—" I start to say.

"No!" she interrupts. "You're going so fast you aren't paying attention. This is NOT going well. We're making it worse. I already sent the SOS to Mr. Valor."

"Oooh—I bet I can fix it before he gets here!" I say, holding up the blue luxolyte so she can see it. "This is going to work! Don't worry! And it's going to be awesome! See you in a sec!"

I hotfoot it up the Great Spiral Monument, hoping I can get there before the Shadow's Shadow reaches the top.

I take off the lid of the jar and throw the powder at him. Success!

Except . . . it doesn't happen the way I thought it would.

It's awful.

AAAAGHHH!

I'm frozen in place, and just then, I hear two things at once: someone's footsteps running up the stairs, and the familiar rocket-engine sound of a jet pack coming down from above.

Tana and Vin Valor arrive at the same moment, but I can't stop staring at the pile of what used to be the Shadow's Shadow.

"I guess I owe you an apology," Tana says in surprise. "You actually captured him!"

"Incredible!" says Vin Valor, his eyes wide.

"Is he . . . is he dead?" I stammer.

"No, no." Valor waves a hand. "At our new super prison, we have incredible ways of restraining and studying villains, and we can easily piece them back together as needed. No worries—we'll still be able to properly interrogate him!"

That wasn't exactly my worry, but *whew.*

If blue luxolyte is so dangerous, what was Mom doing with it? Vin Valor studies me, and I have the weird feeling that maybe he can read my mind.

Yeah. Maybe I won't tell him exactly how much of it really *was* luck.

"That was some serious superheroing . . . um . . ." Vin Valor frowns. "What was your name again? The Amiable Mover?"

"The Amazing *Meower*," corrects Tana.

"No, it's the Stupendous Switcheroo," I say, finally remembering how to talk again. "It just . . . took a little figuring out."

"Yes indeed, sometimes it all just takes a little figuring out," Vin Valor says with a smile. He puts a hand on my back, and suddenly I want to give him a hug.

And also . . . I feel calmer than I have all day.

Which is when I realize that *I am having a casual conversation with Vin Valor,* and since his whole thing is helping people, maybe he can help *me.*

"Er . . . can I ask you a question?"

He raises his eyebrows.

"My mom has been missing. Maybe it's nothing, but I'm starting to worry? And I think you might know her since she's also a scientist?"

Her name is Lilith?

"*Lilith?*" he says. "You're Lilith's kid?"

"Um . . . yes?"

"Wow . . . WOW." He looks at me like he's seeing me for the first time. "It's so obvious now. The blue luxolyte! And you have her eyes!"

I do. The fact that *he* knows that makes me happy in a very specific kind of way. But he hasn't answered my real question yet.

"Absolutely." Vin Valor smiles. "We'll work out the details later. But right now, I need to get back."

"Here you go, sir." Tana hands her boss a sack with all the pieces of the Shadow's Shadow. Just looking at the bag makes me a little woozy.

I ignore the feeling, though, and wave goodbye as Vin Valor gives us a solemn nod and jets away. The moment he leaves, I sink down to the ground.

"Are . . . are you okay?" Tana asks.

I shrug. "I should be *great*. I'm officially on Team Valor! But, I guess—I was hoping he might know something about my mom. "And maybe you didn't notice, but my power of the day is super speed . . ."

"I noticed," she says, sitting next to me.

"And everything's been going so fast," I say. "Too fast. I messed up. I . . . almost killed the Shadow's Shadow. At least, I really hurt him. That's not usually what happens, right?"

"No . . . ," she says, thinking. "But a lot of things aren't happening like usual lately."

"What do you mean?"

"Hacked? *You?*"

"I *know,*" Tana says. "It's infuriating and I can't figure out how they did it. It shouldn't have been possible. They got through the VTech firewall, then my *personal* firewall, they decrypted my encryption, and then . . . downloaded all my email contacts."

"And you don't even know who it is?" I ask.

"No idea. And there was so much top-secret VTech info in the lab drive. Why wouldn't they take that stuff instead? Why break into my personal drive?"

I guess I *should* tell her about the email I got from Suxjr, even if it doesn't mean anything, but before I can, Tana stands up. "I should get back," she says briskly. "Paperwork."

She's so busy, I decide not to mention the email. After all, it's either spam or the wrong address—no reason to worry her for nothing.

And anyway, I can't wait to get home and tell everybody my big news!

"Disagreements about the teleporter?" I ask, and Al gives me a weary look. "Wait—you guys can't understand each other, right? Like, you haven't developed superpowers, have you, Al?"

"I don't mind taking over teleport duty," I volunteer.

After all, it's because of me that Mr. Meatballs is here. And honestly, I kind of *like* having the furball around.

He helps the house feel less empty.

I shake off that thought and get to work on the third mystery of the day. The biggest one. The one that's stared me in the face all day.

Mom.

What is she doing?

Why does she have super dangerous substances lying around?

I go back to the secret lab and start reading her villain files. And right away, I see something that makes all the hairs on my arms stand up.

MR. SUCKO

PERSONAL DETAILS:
Marital status: Married
Children: 1

One kid? ONE KID?

DID I JUST FIGURE OUT WHO SUXJR IS??????????

I mean, I think I did. Suxjr. Sucko Jr. Is that possible? I think back. The email said, *Stay away from my dad.* And I was trying to capture Mr. Sucko right before the email came.

It makes so much sense!

And also it makes no sense.

Suddenly, I can't stand not knowing so many things.

And I really, really, *really* need the one person who COULD figure it all out, who could tell me what's up with my powers, and why there's a secret lab, and what Mr. Sucko's kid is doing emailing me. I need my mom.

I'm done waiting.

You yelled?

We need Mom.

Of course we do. She is a very important part of this family.

No, I mean, we need Mom **now**.

Well, I can try calling again--

We need to teleport her back.

Say what?

She always wears her PinPointer.

If you can bring Mr. Meatballs back ten times a day, you can bring Mom back from wherever she is.

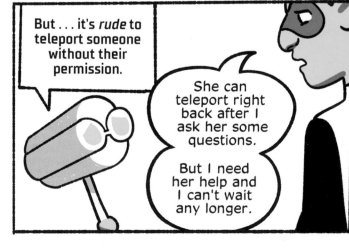

But ... it's *rude* to teleport someone without their permission.

She can teleport right back after I ask her some questions.

But I need her help and I can't wait any longer.

Please.

"I don't like this," Al says. "But to be honest, it would make me feel better if Mom was here, too. So . . . okay."

A couple minutes later, Al is typing into the teleporter controls, and I'm doing a very bad job of being patient.

"Okay," Al finally says. "I've locked onto Mom's Pinpointer. Here we go."

There's the usual *foomp,* but Mom doesn't appear in the room.

"It didn't work," I say.

"Yes," says Al quietly. "It did."

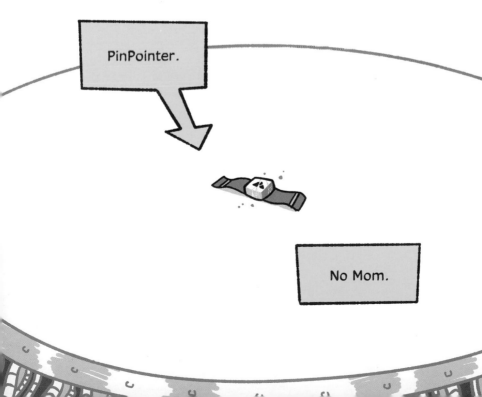

PinPointer.

No Mom.

"Al," I say slowly. "Is it possible that you put in the wrong instructions?"

But I already know the answer is no. Al doesn't make mistakes like that. It's one of the good things about being a robot. Except I still can't understand what I'm seeing.

My mom's Pinpointer. Without my mom.

I don't want to touch it, but Al picks it up.

It looks like it was partly smashed.

The bring-me-back button is mangled.

There's no way Mom could have teleported home unless *we* brought her back.

A chill runs down my spine.

"Why would she take it off? And . . . what if she's in danger?" I ask, even though I don't think I want an answer.

"That's possible," Al says carefully. "But there are plenty of reasonable, non-dangerous explanations."

"I can't think of a single good one," I say, and it's true. My brain is instantly full of every bad thing that could happen to my mom. "All I can think of are sharks and lava and quicksand and all the terrible things there are."

"You know how much she likes volleyball," Al continues. "Maybe she was playing a game and the ball accidentally smashed the Pinpointer. The clasp isn't broken, so she took it off for some reason."

"I guess volleyball is a *little* bit more likely than a shark," I admit.

"We'll keep calling her phone and the hovercar," Al assures me. "She'll probably feel terrible that you were so worried."

Maybe.

But that doesn't make me any less worried.

When I eventually go to bed, I can't sleep. And that makes me wonder . . . if I wake up every morning with a new power, what happens if I stay up all night? Will I still be fast in the morning?

It's very late, and I'm finally starting to get sleepy when I hear the *bing* of my computer telling me somebody sent me an email. At this time of night?

I open it.

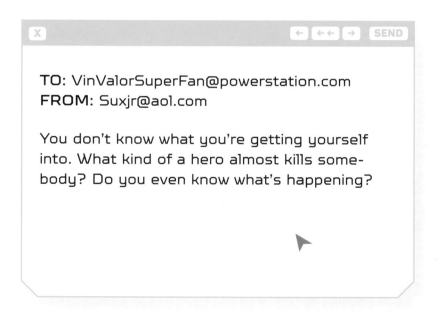

TO: VinValorSuperFan@powerstation.com
FROM: Suxjr@aol.com

You don't know what you're getting yourself into. What kind of a hero almost kills somebody? Do you even know what's happening?

Suddenly, I'm wide awake again.

Suxjr is back—and they know about what happened with the Shadow's Shadow. Even if I'm right about their identity, the truth is I *don't* know what I'm getting myself into and I *don't* know what's happening.

About anything, really.

I think about all the secrets swirling around, and all the mysteries.

Too many of both.

The next thing I know, I wake up on the floor, Mr. Meatballs sprawled out beside me. I guess I could get into bed, but that seems like a lot of work.

I feel myself dozing off again, and the last thing I think is this:

Maybe I don't know what's happening. Not yet.
But I will.

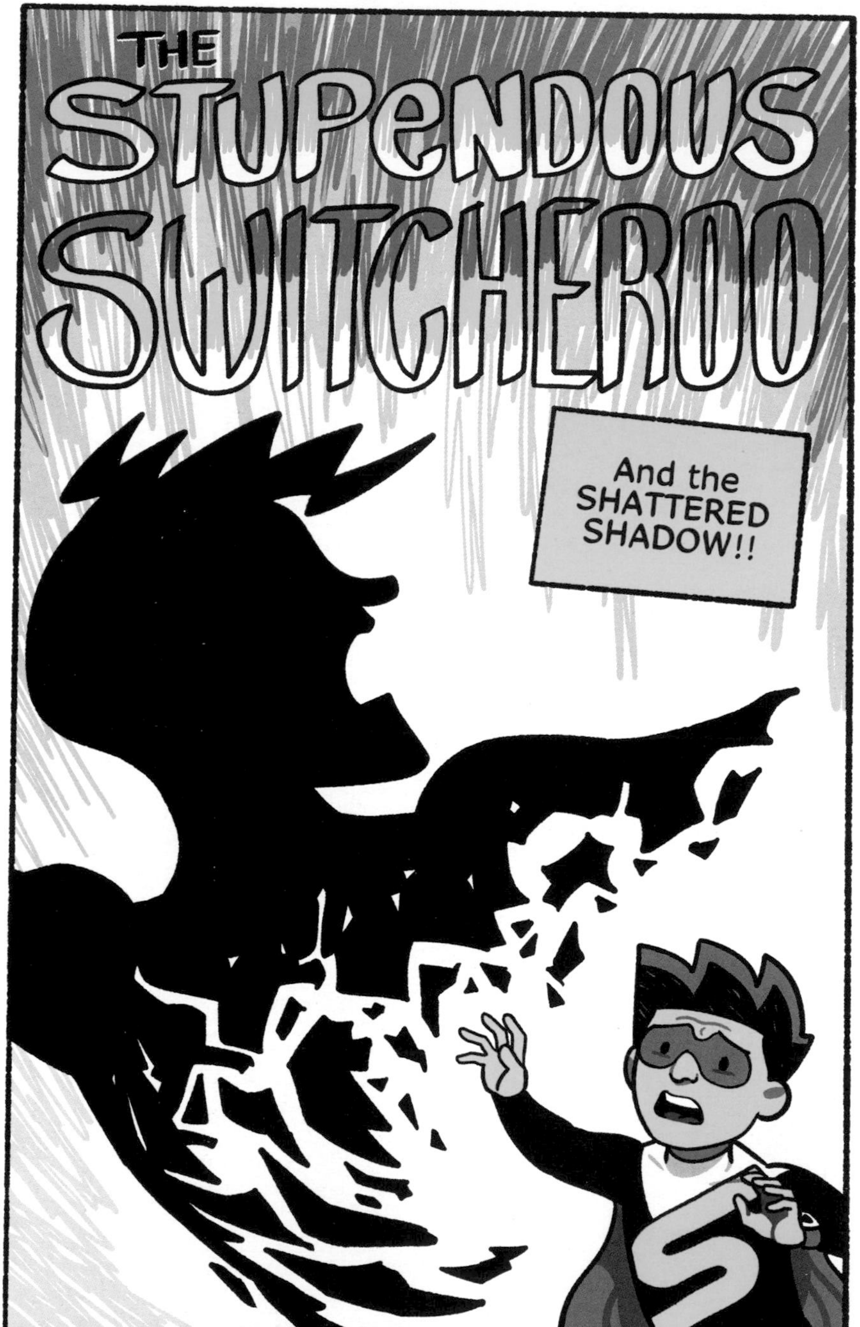
THE
STUPENDOUS
SWITCHEROO
And the SHATTERED SHADOW!!

CHAPTER 5

When I wake up the next morning, the first thing I want to do is test to see if I kept any of my super speed. I didn't stay up *all* night, but I *did* stay up pretty late.

So I throw all my clothes into the air and zip around, trying to get dressed before they hit the floor. Let's just say . . . it doesn't work.

Definitely no more super speed. Once I get dressed (the right way), I track down Al in the kitchen and we do a power scan to figure out today's power.

"What does *that* mean?" I ask. "How is 'bubbles' a superpower?"

"Maybe it means you can make fizzy water?" Al suggests. "That would be pretty terrific. Mom would really love that power."

We both fall silent for a second, thinking about the damaged Pinpointer. Mom would, in fact, be SO excited about fizzy water, but even if I *could* make it, she isn't here to see it.

Not unless I find her.

"We need a new idea," I say. "The Pinpointer didn't work, calling isn't working—but what if we try to find the hovercar instead? Al, can you locate the hovercar's transponder signal?"

"Negative. I'd have to hack a spy satellite and I don't know how to do that."

"Can you at least *try*?" I ask, throwing my hands in the air as bubbles come out of my fingertips.

Um. *Bubbles come out of my fingertips.*

Okaaaay.

Looks like I figured out today's superpower. The bubbles don't seem too dangerous, but at least they're pretty?

I take back what I said about them not being dangerous.

But I won't let the bubbles distract me. "Al, could you just *try* to hack the satellite? It would be a huge help."

Al just shrugs. "I simply don't have the technical capacity."

"You can make scrambled eggs, sew superhero costumes, and read all my email, but you can't do one little teeny, tiny satellite hack?"

Tana said her email got hacked. Then I got those messages. I could be wrong, but I think that means . . . Suxjr is a hacker.

I have a real chance at getting into that satellite—if I can just convince Suxjr to help me. And based on those emails . . . I'm guessing that might not be easy.

"Excuse me!" I yell to Al, and slide all the way to my room on the soapy floor. When I get to my computer, I pull up my email.

TO: Suxjr@aol.com
FROM: VinValorSuperFan@powerstation.com

Dear Suxjr,

Thanks for your emails. I don't know how you found out what happened with the Shadow's Shadow, but you're right. It wasn't good.

Honestly, I don't think I DO know what's happening.

And I could use some help.

Any chance we could meet in person? Nobody else knows about this email (except my robot, who reads my email . . . it's complicated).

Sincerely,
The Stupendous Switcheroo

I hit send—and one second later, I hear Al yell from somewhere in the house. "I don't think that's a good idea!"

"Too late!" I yell back, but suddenly I'm very, very nervous. I need this to work. But there are so many things that could go wrong, starting with what if Suxjr just ignores the emai—

BING.

Oh. Oh wow. My hand is shaking as I open the brand-new message from Suxjr. There's nothing but some coordinates. And the word *today*. So . . . I'm supposed to go wherever that is, today.

Am I really going to do this?

Okay, fine, I'm still a little nervous. It would definitely be better if my power was a bit more . . . serious today. But I'm going to do whatever it takes to find Mom.

And that's what I tell Al.

> **Absolutely not.**

> **You're worried, too. You can't pretend you aren't.**

> **That may be, but--**

> **We're probably the only people who even know she's missing!**

I'm impatient to go meet Suxjr, but Al putters back and forth, making a sort of clinkering noise that I suspect is robot for *This is a bad idea, a really bad idea, why do we always have to do your bad ideas.*

After a minute, though, the clinkering stops. "Okay, fine," Al says. "But you teleport back here the instant something goes wrong."

Oh. Right.

For a split second, I wonder if I should ask her for help, but no. I need this to stay under the radar. Even Tana's radar.

Plus, if I told her about this meeting, I'd also have to tell her that I lied to her about the email from Suxjr, and, well, that would be . . . complicated.

No, I need to handle this myself.

I get into the teleporter. Al doesn't say anything to me, but I'm pretty sure we're both thinking the same thing: *Hope it's not a trap.*

VIN VALOR #1 FAN CLUB CLUBHOUSE

????

FOOOMP

This seems okay.

And doesn't look at all like a—

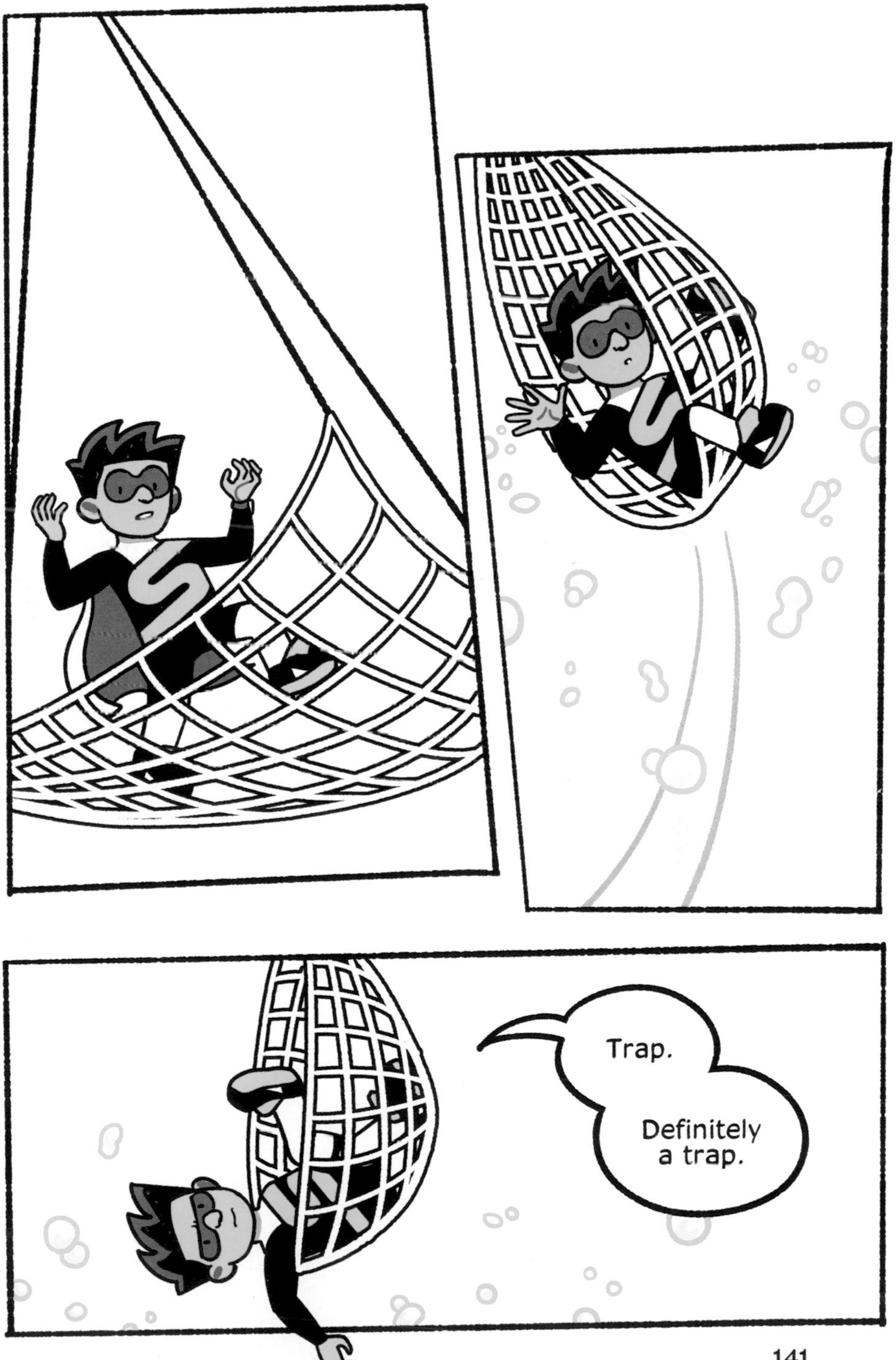
Trap.
Definitely a trap.

I wait there for a second listening to the sound of bubbles popping around me. If I'm right, Suxjr is going to be here any minute.

The door of the clubhouse creaks open.

Turns out I am very right.

VIN VALOR #1 FAN CLUB CLUBHOUSE

Definitely see the Sucko family resemblance.

"Well?" she growls.

"Hi!" I say, trying to sound like a person who deserves to not be trapped in a net. "I'm the Stupendous Switcheroo! You must be Suxjr! SO nice to meet you!" I stick my arm out to shake her hand.

"I really am sorry," I apologize. "I'm not that good at the bubbles yet. Also, careful—they're slippery."

"Hmph," she says.

I'm getting the feeling she might not be the kind of person who slips. Or even just makes mistakes in general.

And *of course* I'm getting a cramp in my neck from the whole trap thing. "It's a bit uncomfortable up here . . . Any chance you might let me down?"

"How do I know I can trust you?" she asks.

Because, um... to be honest...

Technically speaking, I could have teleported out of here the moment it happened.

"But I stayed," I continue, "because I really want to talk. Really."

She looks around, sighs, and then, using some complicated-looking ropes and pulleys, lowers me to the ground.

"I thought you'd look more like Mr. Sucko," I blurt out.

"I'm only half vacuum," she says. "My mom's the Lightning Bolt. Not that it's any of your business."

"I never really thought about Mr. Sucko having a family," I admit.

"No kidding."

I bite my lip. "See, I was helping Vin Valor—"

"Helping him what, be a hero?" she scoffs. "If you're supposed to be such a hero, why are you helping put all my friends' parents in jail?"

Did I hear her right?

"What do you mean, all your friends' parents?" I ask.

"Well," she says, sounding annoyed, "just in the last few days, Lou Ooze. The Shadow's Shadow."

"Well, first of all," I say, "your dad was *robbing a bank*. That's pretty basic villain stuff."

"He went in to get a loan! He's trying to hire a lawyer to get all those 'villains' out of jail. But banks don't want to lend money to a vacuum man."

"So he *stole* all the money instead?"

"Okay, *maybe* he overreacted, but he only did that because the moment he walked in, the security guard started attacking him."

147

"Whatever," she says, gritting her teeth. "It happens all the time. Dad took the money so he could afford to get a big-time lawyer. Everybody else is too chicken to go up against Vin Valor."

I feel terrible for her.

But I also know Vin Valor. He's just out there being a hero. "There has to be a reason he's putting them in jail. He wouldn't do it for no reason."

"Of course he has a reason," she says.

"What is it?" I ask.

Nobody knows.

All we know is that he built the prison just for people like **us**.

And so far, **nobody's** gotten out.

Shivers run up my spine.

But she's not done. "That's why I wrote you the email. You've got to stop helping Valor. Please."

"So," I say, pointing to the sign on the cabin. "You aren't really his #1 fan, huh?"

"Just a disguise," she says. Then her eyes narrow. "He's a dangerous man."

After a minute, I say, "I need to think it over. This is just a lot. Thank you for trusting me."

"Who says I trust you?" she jokes.

Er . . . at least I *think* it's a joke.

"You should go now," she says. "Email when you have your answer. The others didn't think it was a good idea to talk to you—"

"Wait," I say. "I need your help, too."

She looks at me, startled.

"You're a hacker, right?" I ask. "You hacked into Valor Technologies, which is impossible."

She shrugs. "*Almost* impossible."

"Then why'd you only take Tana's email contacts? Why not the other stuff?"

Maybe I already had it.

You're a **super** hacker.

Possibly.

I need you to hack something for me.

"Okaaaay." She studies me. "I'm not saying I can. Or that I will. But tell me more."

"My mom is missing."

Her eyebrows shoot up.

"She hasn't been in touch for two weeks. That's not like her. There's nothing else my robot can do. And . . . I think she may be in some kind of trouble."

"So what could a hacker do to help? *If* somebody actually *was* a hacker."

"I want to locate her car. I mean, her . . . um . . . hovercar. And to do that, I need to hack into a spy—"

"—satellite." She finishes my sentence for me. "That sounds like a challenge."

And I like a challenge.

"So you'll do it?"

"I'll do it," she says, smiling. "IF . . ."

"If what?"

"If you tell me what's up with those bubbles. Where's your fancy super speed? Your telekinesis?"

"Right . . . ," I say, trying to figure out how to explain. "The bubbles. Well . . . every day I wake up with a different power. Today, it's bubbles, apparently. Usually I practice a little, but I was sort of in a rush this morning."

It's the nicest thing she's said to me this whole time.

Then, to my surprise, she opens the door behind her and waves me in. "I need her name and any details you can give me on the vehicle. And don't touch *anything* in here. In fact, while I'm working on that satellite, why don't you practice your bubbles?"

The inside of the cabin is dark and shadowy. There are a couple of ratty sofas and chairs in the middle. A few doors lead to other rooms, except they're all closed. In one corner, a blanket is draped over some old furniture. Suxjr said not to touch anything, but there's not much for me to touch, frankly.

Or that's what I think until she removes the blanket.

Whoa.

We both get to work, but I've only spent a few minutes on my bubbles when—

"Seriously?" I stop mid-bubble. "Already? You're amazing!"

She smiles big, and for a second, I feel like we're old friends. And then I remember that she's the kid of a villain (probably), and I'm a soon-to-be-superhero-sidekick (hopefully), and this could get complicated very fast.

"I'm emailing you the location," she says.

"Thanks," I say. "And I'm going to investigate everything you said. Figure out what's happening at Valor Tech."

"Thank *you*," she says. "And just so you know, my name isn't actually Suxjr—that's just my email. It would be a terrible name. My name is Gasket."

"It was very nice to meet you, Gasket," I say, and make one last bubble.

"Not bad," she says with a grin. "Now, you should *really* go before somebody else gets here."

She doesn't have to tell me twice—I'm so excited about finding Mom, I teleport back home in a blink.

Al! AL!!!!!!!!

Al comes zipping into the teleport room. "Is there a prob—"

"Look at my email. Put those coordinates into the teleporter—it's the location for Mom's hovercar!"

"I'm on it," Al says, immediately typing into the coordinate pad. "Okay. All set."

I'm coming, Mom, I think, and cross my fingers as I teleport away again.

FOOMP

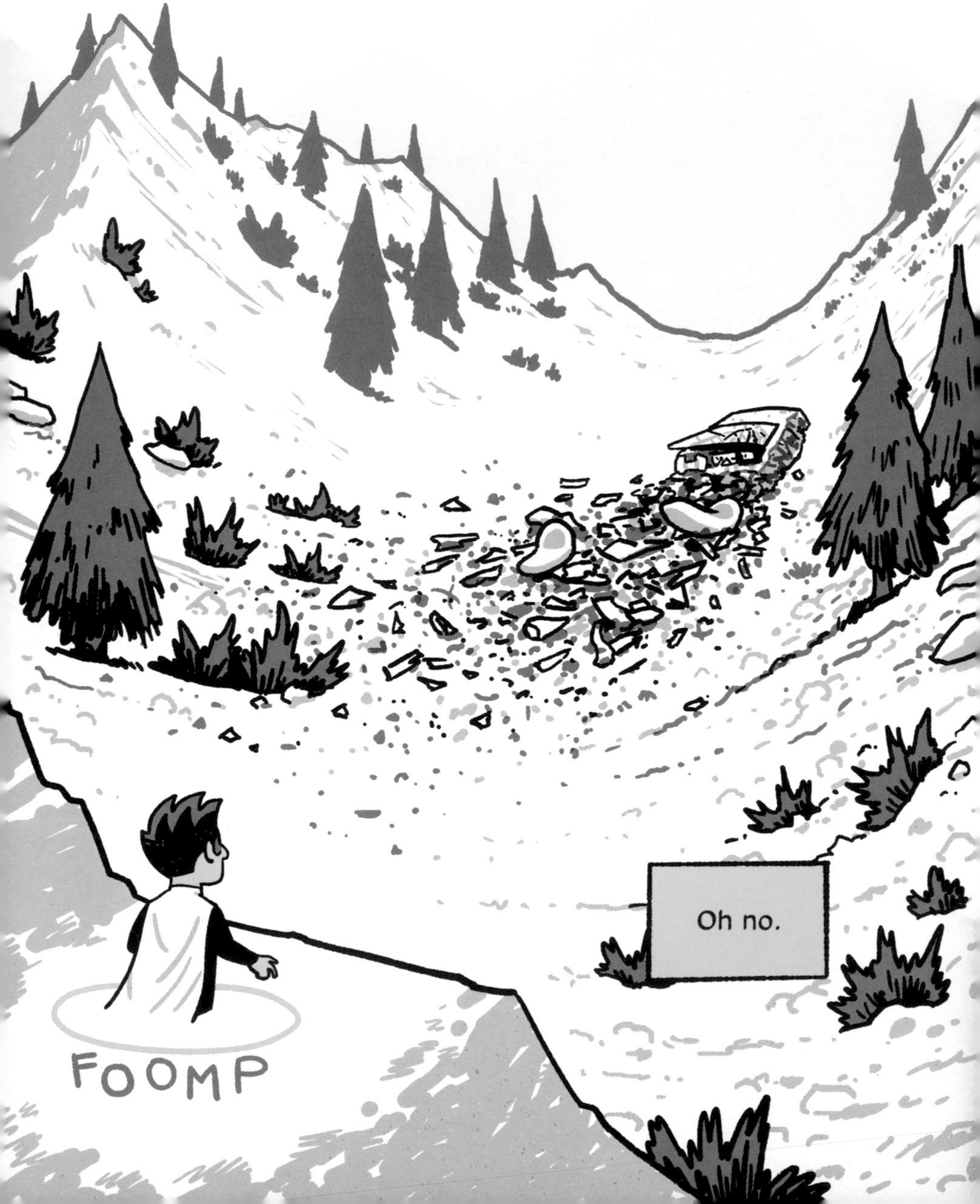
Oh no.
FOOMP

For a minute, I try to convince myself that this isn't Mom's hovercar.

That something else crashed here.

But it's no use.

I'd recognize her hovercar anywhere, even in a million pieces.

I walk around the wreckage, trying to find something, anything that might tell me what happened. But all I see are lumps of twisted metal. Everything looks the same.

MOM?!?

I don't know how long I spend walking around the wreck. When I finally teleport back home, I feel like I'm all hollowed out.

Al makes spaghetti for dinner, but I'm not hungry. And anyway, Al forgets to boil the noodles first, so it's not even really edible.

The two of us sit in the kitchen nook with uncooked noodles on the table and worry about what's happened to Mom.

Al tries to distract me and even takes the parental controls off the Pinpointer, saying how good I've gotten at the teleporter. Any other time, I'd be so happy. But I know it's just because Al's scared, too. Neither of us knows what to do.

At some point, I head to bed. My computer bings— there's a message from Gasket, asking if I found anything at the location. I can't bring myself to reply, so I just close my email.

I almost think knowing about the crash is worse than not knowing anything. Except . . . Mom has to be okay. She made it out of the crash, somehow. So where is she now?

I *am* going to find her.

There's always tomorrow.

THE STUPENDOUS SWITCHEROO

Introducing...
GASKET!

Is she
FRIEND
or FOE?

And...
The Mystery on
the Mountain!

CHAPTER 6

So, okay, the crash site may have been a dead end.

But now it's a brand-new day! And I can keep working to find Mom if I could just get a *helpful* power. (No offense to the bubbles.)

Al and I sit at a table, and Mr. Meatballs leaps up on top of it.

"I brought this," Al announces, dumping out a jigsaw puzzle. "So you can work on your power."

Mr. Meatballs immediately knocks a puzzle piece onto the floor.

"Al." I frown. "I'm not going to play games while Mom is missing."

"Okay, but—"

"I'm serious. I can't sit around and not do anything."

"I wouldn't say you aren't doing anything," Al says, pointing at the table. "You just solved the whole puzzle."

"Al . . ." I force out the words. "I wasn't trying to solve the puzzle."

"You solved it by mistake?"

"No, I mean, *I wasn't even trying.* I'm not *regular* good at doing puzzles—I'm *superhero* good at them. Which means . . ."

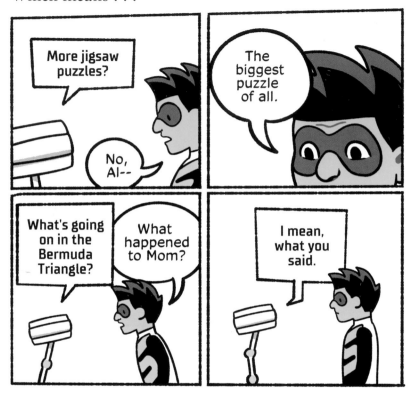

"I need to get back to that crash site," I say. "I couldn't find any clues yesterday, but with this power—it's game on."

A few minutes later, I'm standing in the middle of the wreckage again. It's still awful—but this time, I have a new secret power.

Hope.

And also, doing jigsaw puzzles.

I walk around slowly, picking up pieces of the wreck and putting them down where they belong.

I'm not sure how this works, but it feels almost like having an extra sense—I have this feeling deep in my bones that something just *fits*.

Or . . . that it doesn't.

It's weird. As I move around, I start to notice that some of the metal doesn't belong.

Some pieces aren't part of the hovercar at all.

Pieces that don't fit.

Could they be the key to the whole puzzle?

I've never teleported anything but myself (not counting Mr. Meatballs), so I fiddle with the Pinpointer.

I hear some anxious beeping and look over to see Al staring at the reconstructed hovercar. I understand. It's scary, knowing Mom was in there.

"You did a very good job putting it back together," Al finally manages.

"Thanks," I say. "Now we just need to piece together what happened."

We split up. Al takes a look at the hovercar to see if there's any stored data that might help, while I study the small pile of extra metal.

They aren't all part of the same thing.

These are three different somethings.

Three different...

WHAT???!!!!

"Al," I say. "Is there any reason Mom would have had VTech Vrones in the hovercar with her?"

"No," Al says and then notices the Vrones. "What—what are they doing here?"

It doesn't make sense. Vin Valor said he hadn't seen Mom in years. Is it possible the hovercar and the Vrones just . . . had an accidental midair collision? "I don't know," I say. "But I need to talk to Tana."

I send her a message asking if I can come see her. She sends back her coordinates, and—

AHHH!!

Guess I should've told her I was coming **now**.

FOOMP

"Sorry," I say, helping her clean up the papers.

"Did you ever think of *knocking*?" she says, still a little flustered. "I mean SERIOUSLY, you know teleporting is NOT NORMAL, right? And has anybody ever told you that the way you pop into places is, like, a *huge* security issue?"

"Not yet," I say with a big smile.

She rolls her eyes, *just* a little. "So what's up?"

I lay out two of the Vrones on her desk.

I found these... at the scene of an accident.

Whoa.

Vrones are my **specialty**.

I know **every single kind** of Vrone that VTech makes.

So?

So I've never **seen** this model.

Whatever they **do**...

"I need to find out what happened in that accident," I say, trying not to sound freaked out. "Can you tell if they recorded video or anything?"

She turns over one of the Vrones. "I'm not sure I should—"

"Aren't you a little curious?"

"I don't have clearance for this," she says, prying open a panel. Her eyes widen. "On the other hand, Mr. Valor likes us to take initiative . . ." She looks up sharply. "This doesn't have to do with all the questions he's been asking, does it?"

"No! Wait. What questions?"

"Usually, he asks questions *before* somebody joins Team Valor. But he's been asking questions about you nonstop since you talked at the Great Spiral Monument. Like, *a lot* of questions."

Huh. If Vin Valor has questions about me, why wouldn't he just . . . ask *me*? I can't explain it, but it makes me feel strange.

Especially on top of these secret Vrones.

Tana looks at me sideways. "What aren't you telling me?"

There's SO MUCH I'm not telling her--

Because I don't know how it fits together yet.

It's **so much** more complicated than a jigsaw puzzle.

There's Mom, Gasket...

What's happening to the villains at the jail?

Who can I **trust**?

I really, **really** want to trust Tana.

"I'm not telling you everything," I confirm. "But I hope I can soon."

She looks unsure, but nods.

"Oh, by the way," she says, and pulls a phone out of a drawer. "Mr. Valor insisted."

"It's standard issue for Team Valor," she says with a shrug. "Everybody at VIA—the Valor Innovations Academy—has one."

"Wait—can I call Vin Valor with this?"

She shakes her head. "It's just for *us* to call *you*. Mr. Valor's busy with the whole 'being a tech genius while also running a school to train an army of heroes like himself to make the world safer' thing."

I get it—but being on Team Valor isn't exactly how I imagined it. We're just not that much of a *team*. I head home, leaving the Vrones with Tana and trying not to feel weird about all those questions Vin Valor was asking about me.

He's Vin Valor. My hero. It's fine.

I do feel a *little* bad not telling Tana about the third Vrone. But until I know what's going on, I need all the help I can get. So, once I'm back home, I start a quick email to Gasket and ask if she'll take a look. If Tana can't help, maybe Gasket can hack into it. Before I can hit send, my new phone buzzes with a text.

TG   MR. SUCKO + SIDEKICK. HOSTAGE.

Oh *NO*. I get the location from Tana, and can't stop worrying about Gasket—was she wrong about her dad? There's no time to waste. I teleport over.

It's just as bad as I thought it would be.

Oh, wait. It's WORSE than I thought.

"Calm down, everybody!" I yell. "Let's just talk it out! We can solve this peacefully!" Except nobody can hear me because there's so much commotion from the very recognizable roar of a jet pack.

Vin Valor swoops heroically in front of Mr. Sucko and talks into a megaphone.

YOU WON'T GET AWAY THIS TIME, SUCKO!

I'VE ALREADY GROUNDED THE BLIMP!

I wonder if he's going to pull out a net . . . but then a Vrone appears on either side of him. Out of nowhere. I squint to see them more clearly and realize they're the same version as the ones I found at the crash.

They were stealth tech.

Invisible.

Maybe Mom never even saw them.

But before I can figure out what that means, the Vrones dart toward Mr. Sucko.

DAAAAD!!!!!

"Did you recognize those Vrones?" I ask Tana, but she's not paying attention to me.

She's busy typing into her wrist thingy and doesn't even look up to say, "We've got to catch the sidekick."

Which of course is when Gasket turns around and spots me standing in the street. "Switcheroo?"

Now Tana's *definitely* paying attention to me. *"You know her?"*

Why is everything so complicated?

"You take care of the lawyer," I quickly say to Tana, nudging her in his direction. "Get him to safety and I'll take care of the sidekick!"

Tana frowns, but she turns toward the lawyer as I run toward Gasket.

I don't know exactly how, but Gasket's an important piece of the puzzle. I can't let her get caught. I don't want anything to happen to her.

So I run at her full speed, reaching for my Pinpointer—

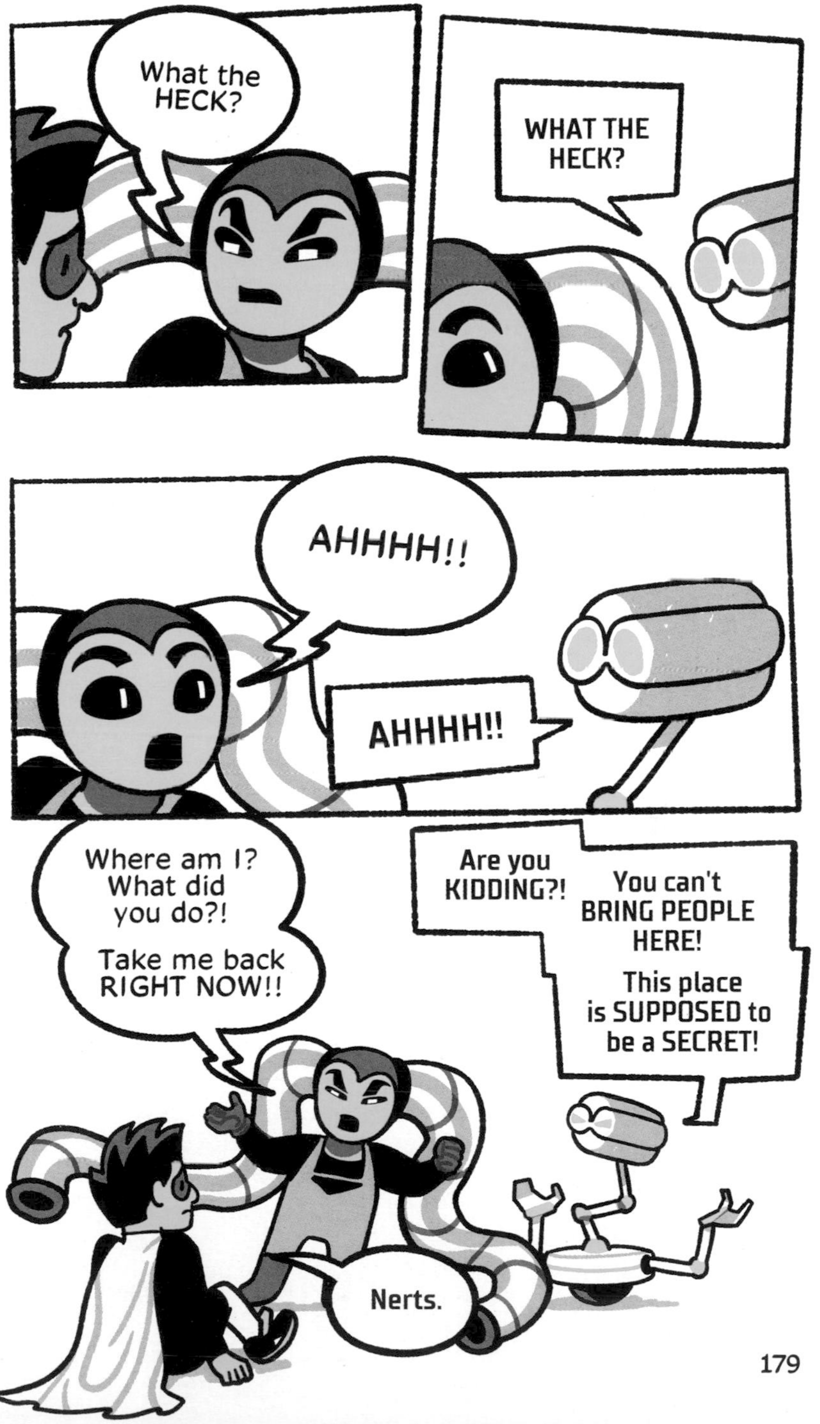
What the HECK?
WHAT THE HECK?
AHHHH!!
AHHHH!!
Where am I? What did you do?!
Take me back RIGHT NOW!!
Are you KIDDING?!
You can't BRING PEOPLE HERE!
This place is SUPPOSED to be a SECRET!
Nerts.

"Okay," I say when they take a break from yelling. "I get it, you both think this was a bad idea."

"But," I continue, "it was the only solution. Gasket, you were in danger."

"Danger? My DAD is in danger!" she yells. "My dad! Because Vin Valor has him! And I need to get back there and save him!"

"There's nothing you can do," I say with a sigh. "I know you were trying to help, but Vin Valor almost put you in jail, too. We need to figure out a way to explain to him that there's been a misunderstanding— but this isn't the moment."

"Speaking of being helpful," Al pipes in, "maybe you could be *really* helpful and teleport her right back out of here."

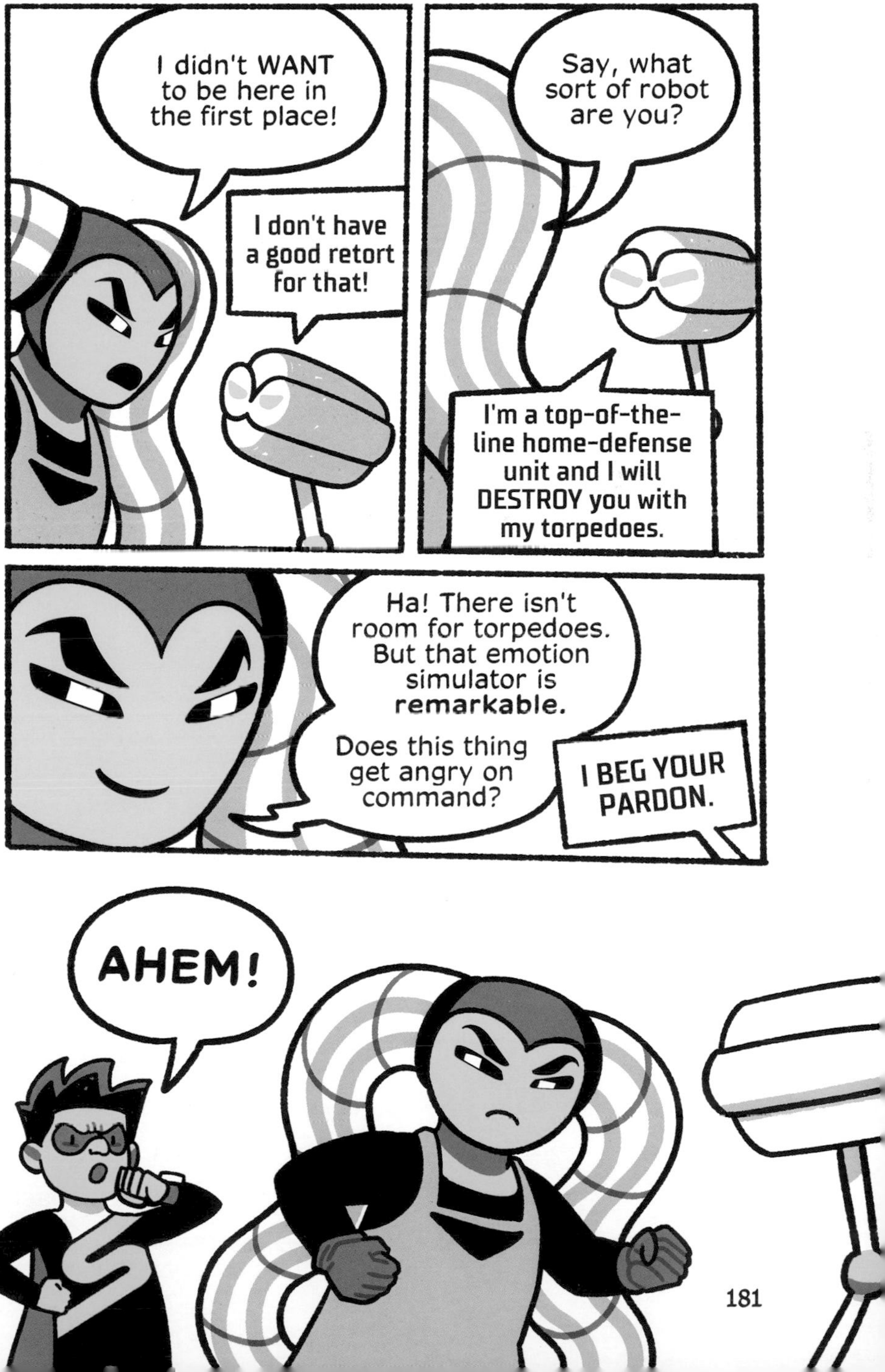
I didn't WANT to be here in the first place!
I don't have a good retort for that!
Say, what sort of robot are you?
I'm a top-of-the-line home-defense unit and I will DESTROY you with my torpedoes.
Ha! There isn't room for torpedoes. But that emotion simulator is remarkable.
Does this thing get angry on command?
I BEG YOUR PARDON.
AHEM!

"Gasket, er . . . maybe I should take you home?" I say.

She looks at Al one more time and nods. "But not home. The clubhouse. Where we met in the woods." We hop in the teleporter (although of course she has to study that, too), and moments later, we're back at her cabin.

"That's an impressive robot, but there's something off about it," she says distractedly.

I change the subject. "What were you and your dad doing with that lawyer, anyway?"

"My dad made an appointment with that guy. It was part of Dad's plan to get everybody out of jail. But then the lawyer saw him and assumed he was there to cause trouble." She looks away. "You don't know what it's like."

"You sure you're going to be okay?" I ask.

"Yeah," she says gruffly. "We've got a—
Ring ring!

I decide not to mention that Vin Valor insisted that I have it.

"My friend Tana is calling," I explain. "As far as she knows, you and I just disappeared."

"Don't answer." Gasket still looks panicky. "They might be tracking the location."

"I need to tell her what happened."

"*No.*"

She's one of THEM.

But if we give her a chance--

I think she could be one of **us**.

Gasket frowns.

"I mean, I know she's part of VTech," I explain. "But I also think she wants to do what's right."

"You don't know that for sure," Gasket argues. "And until you do, you can't tell her about me. And you can't tell *anyone* about the clubhouse. Seriously. It's bad enough your email-reading robot knows."

She might be right—it's so hard to know for sure. I take a breath and answer the phone.

"I need a status report!" Tana yells into the phone. There are sirens behind her.

"Right, so—"

"*What?*"

I speak louder. "You know how Mr. Sucko is really good at escaping? I guess it runs in the family! Gasket totally got away!"

"Are you saying Mr. Sucko and the sidekick are related? And her name is Gasket???"

Oops. "I think you're breaking up," I say, making staticky noises on the phone. "I'll talk to you later!"

I hang up.

"But thank you for trying, I guess," she says. Her tentacles twist, and I realize she's still worried.

If there's anything I understand, it's being worried about your parent.

"I'm sure your dad's okay," I offer. "Vin Valor mentioned something about interrogating the Shadow's Shadow, so maybe he's just going to talk to your dad and then let him go?"

Gasket shoots me a look. She knows I'm just trying to make her feel better. And it's not working.

I'm going to try to fix this.

ALL of this.

Whatever is really going on.

Thanks.

There isn't anything I can do for her right now, though, so I head back home.

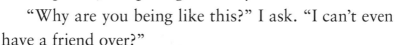

I'm only half surprised to find that Al's in front of the teleporter, still pacing furiously.

"Why are you being like this?" I ask. "I can't even have a friend over?"

Actually, I'm not sure Gasket and I count as friends at this point, but that's a different conversation.

"An AWFUL lot of them," Al mumbles.

I think about what Gasket said—maybe there *is* something wrong with Al. What did she say? *There's something off about that robot.*

I don't see the big deal with ignoring a rule or two, but I don't want to fry any of Al's circuits. And since Al is almost all I've got right now, I guess I should be a little more careful.

"I'm sorry," I say. "No more friends over without talking to you first."

"That is acceptable," Al sniffs.

There's just one small, furry problem with that plan.

"Maybe we can just do the pieces around him?" I suggest.

Al beeps in agreement.

We settle in, and I go slow, so we can fill in the pieces together. It *doesn't* help when Mr. Meatballs stretches and knocks half the pieces off the table.

But that's okay. This puzzle is just for fun.

It's the other puzzle that I can't get out of my head—the mystery of what happened to Mom after the crash.

My jigsaw puzzle power turned out to be great—at least, it's been great when the pieces are right in front of me. But my powers haven't changed one thing: I still don't know how to find Mom.

There are just too many missing pieces.

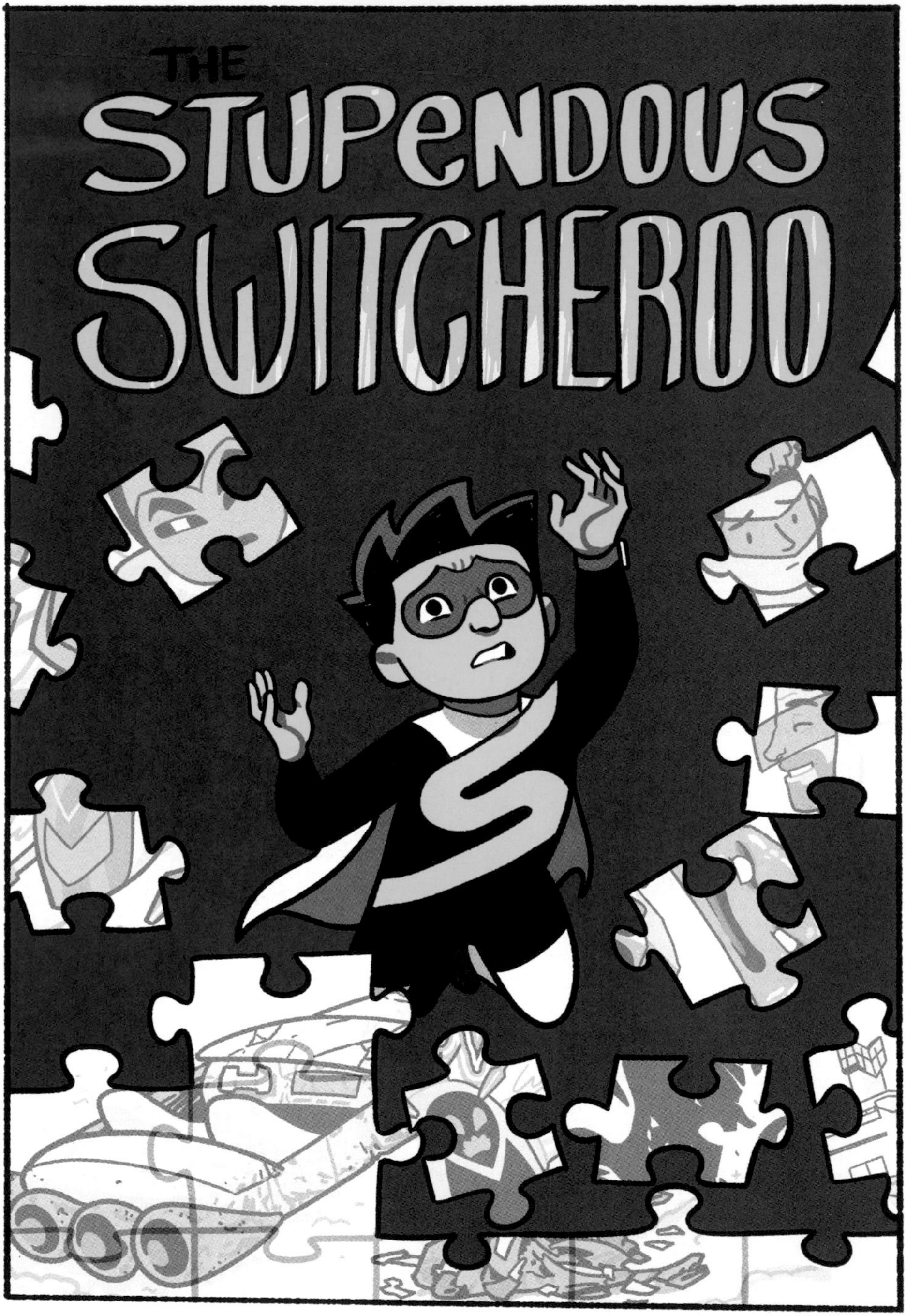
THE
STUPENDOUS
SWITCHEROO

CHAPTER 7

I thought I was getting the hang of having different powers every day.

But the next morning, my power identification scan is very weird.

It says "spiky bones."

That isn't a thing.

It definitely says spiky bones.

What the heck is "spiky bones"?

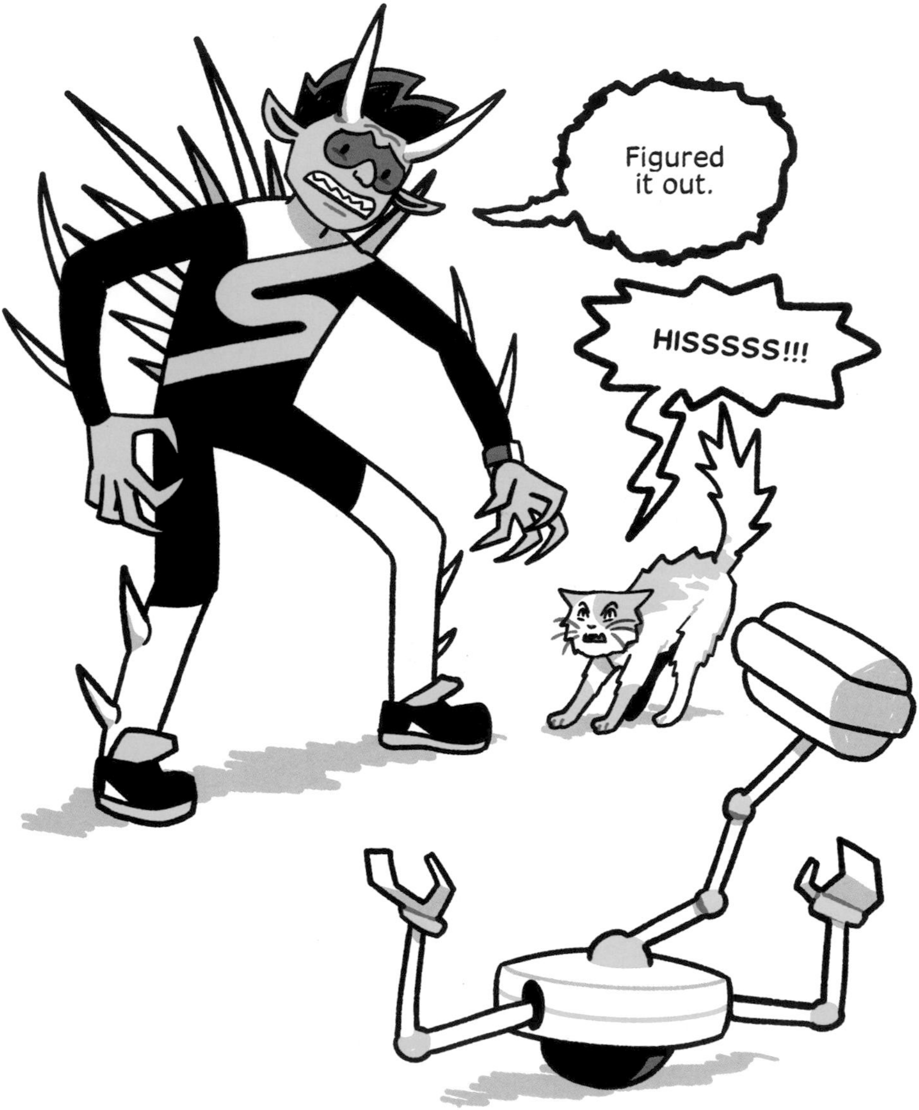
Figured it out.
HISSSSS!!!

"Mr. Meatballs, it's just me!" I call after him, but the cat's already out of sight.

"He'll come around," Al says comfortingly.

I take a breath and try to relax, and slooooowly I change back into myself—until the moment I *stop* relaxing, when I *immediately* transform into spiky bones again. I'm like some kind of monster porcupine.

Just then, one of the spikes shoots off into the air and sticks in the ceiling.

That's not great.

I need a pep talk. "Okay," I say to myself. "This is fine. It's not the weirdest thing that's ever happened to you."

"It's like any other power," I say to Al. "I just need practice."

"If you say so," Al says.

Al goes off to give Mr. Meatballs a treat, while I try to deal with the spiky bones problem. Except just as I start practicing . . .

"Hi," Tana says.

"Hi, Tana! Bet you can't guess my power toda—"

"I saw the security footage from yesterday," she interrupts. "With Mr. Sucko. And his daughter. And *you*. We need to talk."

Oooooh boy—she knows I teleported Gasket away from the crime scene.

And you know what? She's right. We do need to talk. I'm sick of keeping so many secrets.

"I'm feeling a little . . . unpredictable right now," I say. "I'd rather not meet at Valor Tech. How about the park where we captured Lou Ooze?"

She agrees. And *hopefully* I can teleport without changing?

Argh.

I transform back to myself, and then concentrate really hard on *staying* myself.

Tana arrives a few minutes later. "Why are your eyes closed?"

"I'm being very, very calm," I explain.

"Oh," she says. "Sorry about this, then."

Things happen pretty quickly after that.

I transform. AGAIN.

Tana screams.

"I don't need saving!" Tana protests. "I was just surprised!"

The old man doesn't hear her.

And he is *surprisingly* fast.

"Your new power?" Tana asks me as the old man walks away, clearly disappointed he can't keep beating me up.

"Yup," I say, trying to catch my breath.

"Still getting the hang of it?"

"Yup."

"Okay. So less yelling," Tana says agreeably. "Here's the thing. I respect that you have some secrets. But not if they mess this up for me."

There's a **reason** I'm the top student at the Innovations Academy.

I take my VTech work **seriously**.

I understand what she's saying—but it also makes me worry. If I uncover something sinister at Valor Tech, what will Tana do?

But then I hear her voice in my head, from just a second ago. *He's my friend.*

I'm her friend. It's time for me to start trusting her. For real. And hopefully, it won't be a huge mistake.

I think there's something **fishy** going on at Valor Technologies.

"What do you mean, fishy?" Tana frowns.

"I'm not sure. But you know when things just don't feel right?"

She nods.

"Something feels really wrong." I take a deep breath and say what I haven't even been able to admit to myself yet. "Something with Valor Tech and the villains and the super jail. But I don't know what it adds up to or who's behind it."

"I don't think I have any useful intel," she says. "Except maybe . . ."

"Oh, I know!" she says. "I bet he'll be at the press conference!"

"What press conference?"

"Tomorrow. Mr. Valor's holding a ribbon-cutting ceremony at the prison. It's a whole big thing—I bet the mysterious man will be there."

"Well, then," I say. "So will I."

Tana's wrist thingy beeps. "I should get back."

"Just one more thing," I say. "Gasket—Mr. Sucko's daughter—she's not a bad person. She's helping me."

"The Vacuum Danger Tween?? She's *helping*???"

She wants to know the truth, too.

Well, that complicates things.

I know.

It's okay.

We'll figure it out.

Also, wow, Gasket will NOT like that nickname.

"So," Tana says. "What can *I* do?"

Suddenly, I feel like I might melt from relief—*it wasn't a mistake to trust her.*

"Watch out for the mystery man," I suggest. "And keep looking into those stealth Vrones."

With that sneaky tech, they could be anywhere, anytime.

Like the perfect spy machines.

That's not all...

They may have **caused** that crash you were looking into.

Wait. What? I feel like somebody just squeezed all the air out of me.

"I'm not saying it was intentional," she continues, "but based on the impact marks, the Vrones were too close to the hovercar's thrusters."

"And that could have caused the accident?" I ask, feeling numb.

"It's likely." She shrugs. "They might've had a navigational error and flown too close. New technology is always unpredictable."

I can't say anything.

Tana tilts her head to the side. "Where does the crash fit into all this?"

Tana...

My mom was in that crash.

It takes a second before I feel steady. I hadn't planned to tell her about Mom yet.

"Now she's missing," I say when I'm ready. "I don't know how the crash fits into everything. But I think it does, somehow."

"I'm so sorry," Tana says. She hesitates and then continues slowly, as if she's still deciding how much to tell me. "There's . . . a secret database I'm not supposed to know about. When I analyzed those Vrones you brought in, I discovered that they're uploading data to a secret server. That server should have records of any covert missions those Vrones are doing."

"Two villains reported in a hostile situation," she says as the information beeps across her screen. "Professor Boingo and Madam Puff. I'll text you the coordinates."

I've read about them, too, but now I wonder how much of what I've read is real. Tana notices my hesitation.

"Are you coming?" she asks.

"I have to try something first," I say. "But if Vin Valor asks, I'll be there as soon as I can."

I've made it through most of this conversation without any spikes, so I'm hoping I can teleport with no problem.

And I'm *also* hoping that this plan I just came up with doesn't backfire.

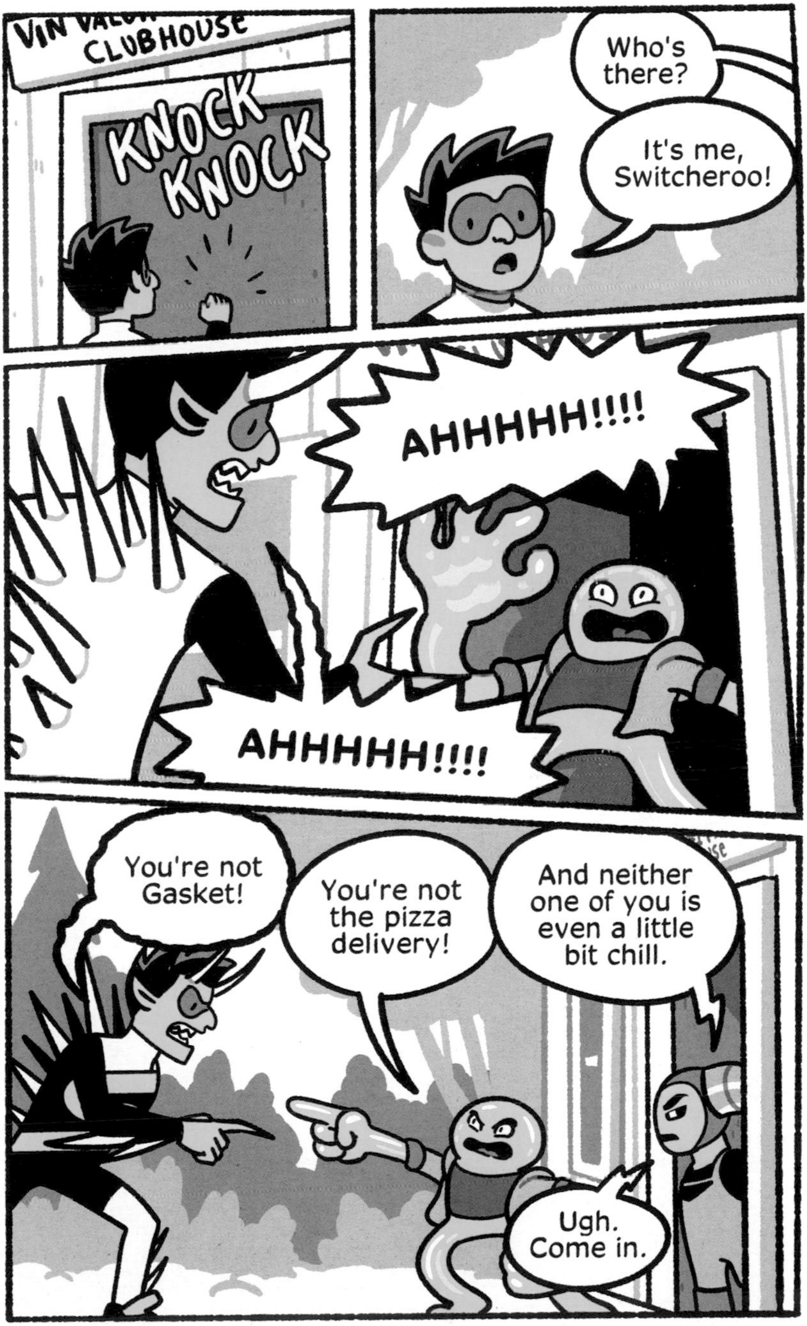

CLUBHOUSE
KNOCK KNOCK
Who's there?
It's me, Switcheroo!
AHHHHH!!!!
AHHHHH!!!!
You're not Gasket!
You're not the pizza delivery!
And neither one of you is even a little bit chill.
Ugh. Come in.

We sit down in the main room, and one by one I get the spikes to go down.

"Weird power," Gasket observes.

"You're telling me," I say.

The other kid stands up and points at me. "He shouldn't be here."

Gasket rolls her eyes a little. "Switch, meet Slimeball. Slimeball, Switch."

"You look familiar," I say. I can't think of where I would have seen him before, though. He's very . . . um . . . slimy? Sort of . . . oozy?

He flounces down on the sofa and glares at Gasket. "I'm not talking to him. He's not in the club, he shouldn't be here."

"I won't stay long," I promise. "Gasket, how do you feel about another hacking job?"

"This is important," I say, interrupting them. "I found out where Valor Tech stores their top-secret data. It's on a secret server."

"Pfft," says Gasket. "I eat secret servers for breakfast."

"You eat . . . really?" I say. "That's not bad for your teeth?" The moment the words are out of my mouth, I realize that she doesn't actually mean *she eats servers*.

In my defense, she looks like she *could*.

When they finish laughing at me, I say, "There's a problem, though. The security is impossible to get through."

"You haven't really seen my powers in action," Gasket says, leaning in. "But there's no such thing as impossible to me. *I am the world's greatest hacker.*"

Suddenly, Slimeball is standing between us. "What if it's a trap!" he snarls, pushing me back.

"If this was a trap"—I can feel myself going full spiky bones—"you'd already be in jail. I want that information as much as you do."

DO you?

There might be information about a hovercar crash in those files!

A crash that **my mom** was in.

So, yeah. I want those files, too.

Slimeball seems a little nicer after that.

I'm about to go when I remember something. "Oh, one more thing. There's another villain situation happening. Professor Boingo and Madam Puff are involved."

"I thought you *wanted* action," I say.

"*Coordinated* action," Gasket says, electrical sparks flying off her. "The adults are making everything worse. They each have their own separate plans: shut down the jail, capture Vin Valor, take over the internet, hold a beauty pageant—they cannot get it together! That's why—"

Slimeball cuts her off. "Stop. He doesn't need to know."

I can tell that the more interested I look, the more Slimeball is going to shut down. So even though I'm curious about what Gasket was going to say, I let it go.

Anyway, I need to meet Tana at that supervillain double whammy and tell her that Gasket's trying to break into the secret server.

"Thanks," I say. Our friendship may be weird, but I'm grateful we're on the same side . . . whichever side that is.

With that, I teleport to the site of the villain trouble, all ready for commotion—except I don't see any trouble. No Professor Boingo. No Madam Puff. No Tana. To be honest, I'm glad there's nothing for me to do. Everything is getting really . . . complicated.

I'm just about to leave when I hear somebody yell. "ANOTHER VILLAIN!!! OVER THERE!!!!!"

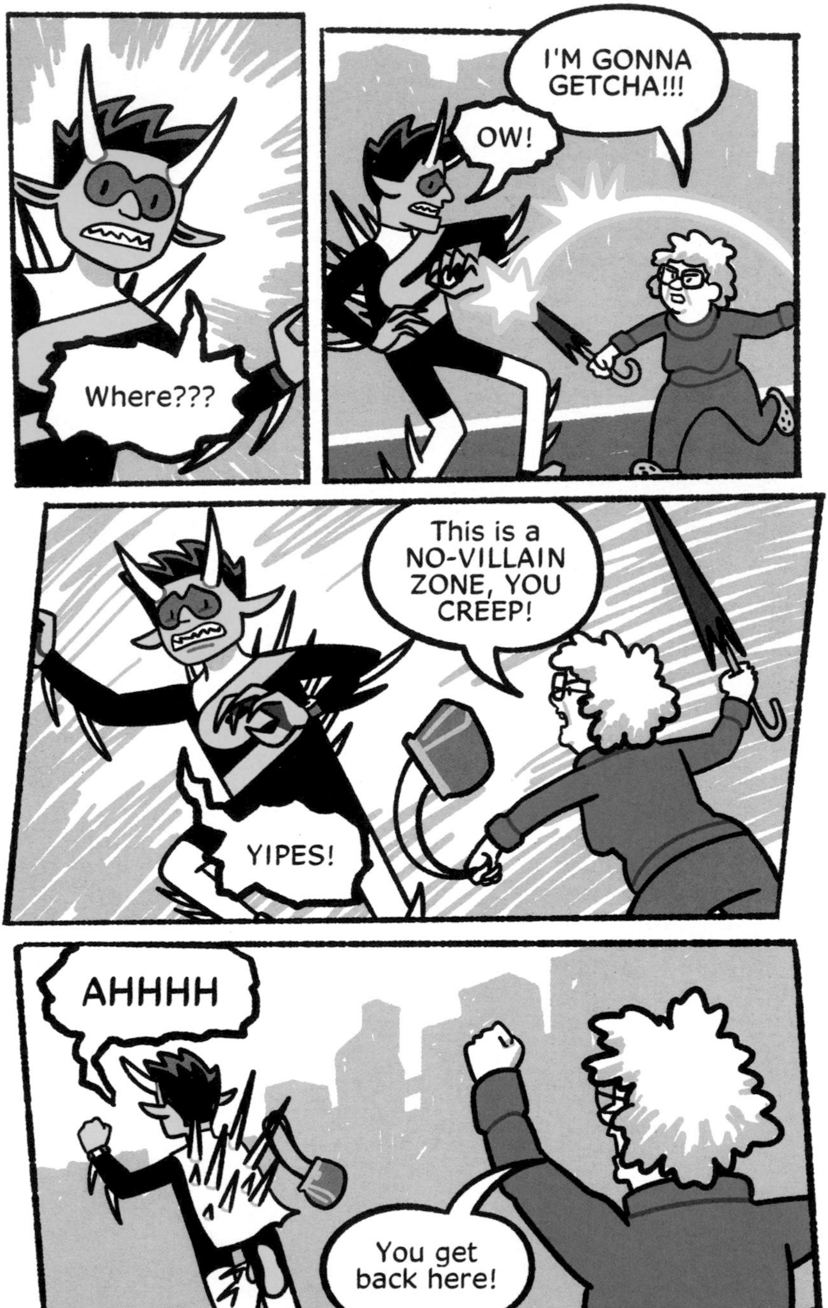
Where???
I'M GONNA GETCHA!!!
OW!
This is a NO-VILLAIN ZONE, YOU CREEP!
YIPES!
AHHHH
You get back here!

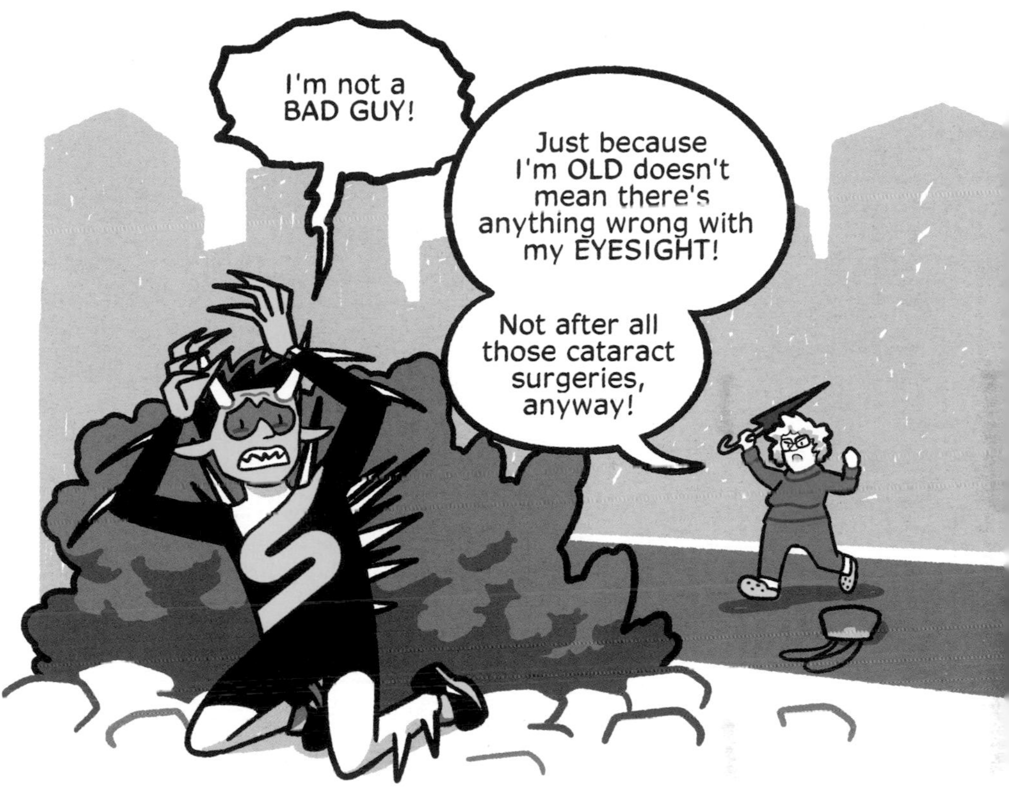
I'm not a BAD GUY!
Just because I'm OLD doesn't mean there's anything wrong with my EYESIGHT!
Not after all those cataract surgeries, anyway!

Why does everybody think I'm a monster? I'm just a kid with huge porcupine spikes. I'm not, like, I don't know . . . a gigantic blob creature . . . or a shadowy menace . . . or . . . a vacuum . . .

Oh.

Suddenly, I understand what Gasket was talking about.

It *does* feel awful to know that somebody is going to look at you and decide you're rotten.

And I did it to those villains. I was exactly like this lady with the umbrella.

No.

I was worse. I'm the reason they're in jail.

Finding Mom is still the most important thing—but I think I just realized how much I owe Gasket and Mr. Sucko and all the rest of them.

An apology is just the beginning.

"Ow!" The fancy umbrella smashes down on my head, and I very quickly decide that I'm not spending any more time looking for Tana.

I get down on the ground, hoping maybe I can convince Mr. Meatballs that I'm not a monster.

"It's just me," I say. "You know me."

He holds up a paw. Claws *out*.

So it's not going that well, apparently.

I pull out my VTech phone and text her.

SS: Sorry I'm so late. What happened with Boingo and Puff?

TG: We took them into custody.

TG: But...

SS: ?

TG: Thinking about what you said

SS: About what

TG: VTech, villains, jail

SS: Gotcha

TG: Also, FYI, VTech got hacked today

SS: WHAT?

TG: Security's been stepped up

I stop and reread her text. There was a hack? *Today?*

That's amazing! Gasket already did it! I know I'll have to be patient (Tana says *everything* there is encrypted), but I'm so excited by the news that I run into the kitchen and bump right into Al.

I don't even care what we have for dinner. All I can think about is those top-secret files!

But it's dinnertime, so I *guess* I should eat. The smell of shish kebab (haha, very funny, Al) fills the kitchen as I sit in the nook and tell Al and Mr. Meatballs about everything that happened today.

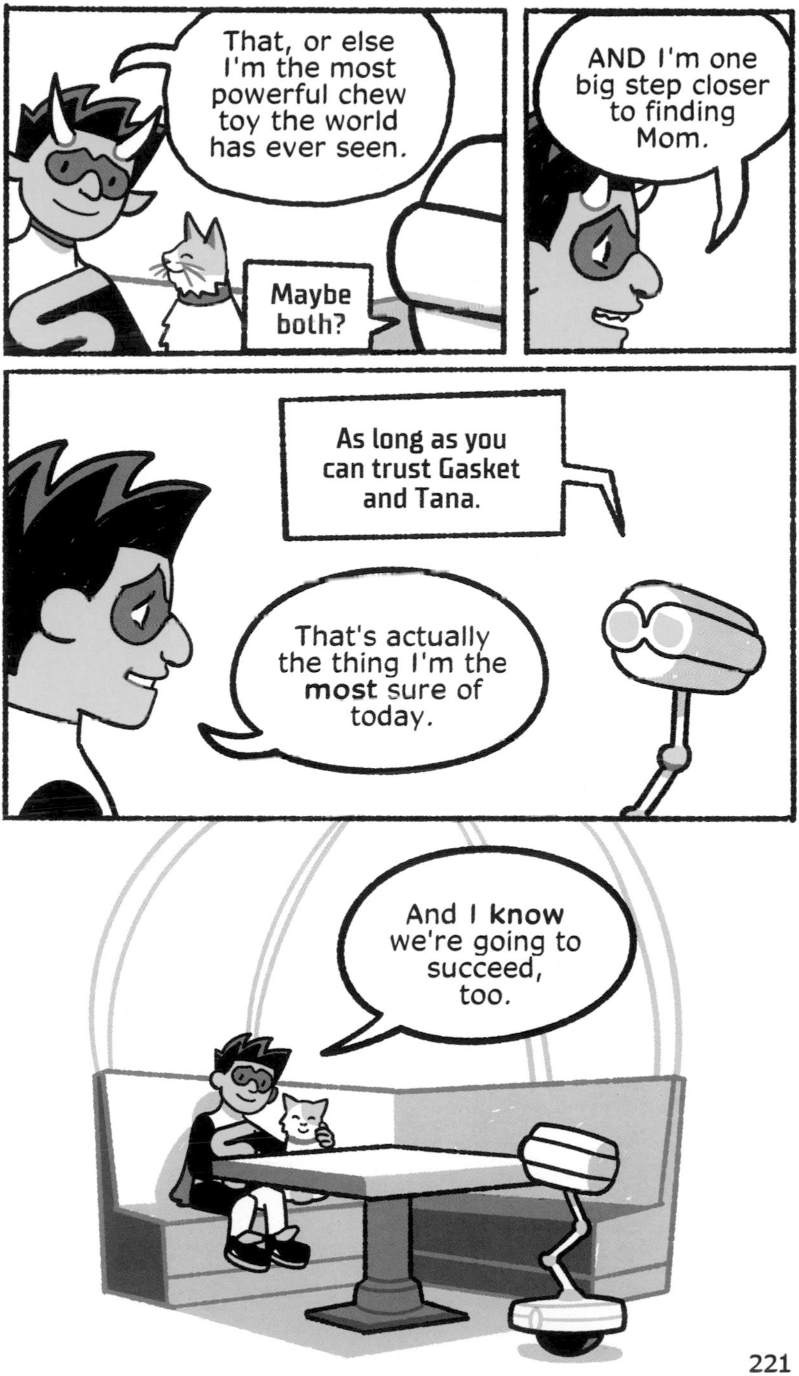
That, or else I'm the most powerful chew toy the world has ever seen.
Maybe both?
AND I'm one big step closer to finding Mom.
As long as you can trust Gasket and Tana.
That's actually the thing I'm the **most** sure of today.
And I **know** we're going to succeed, too.

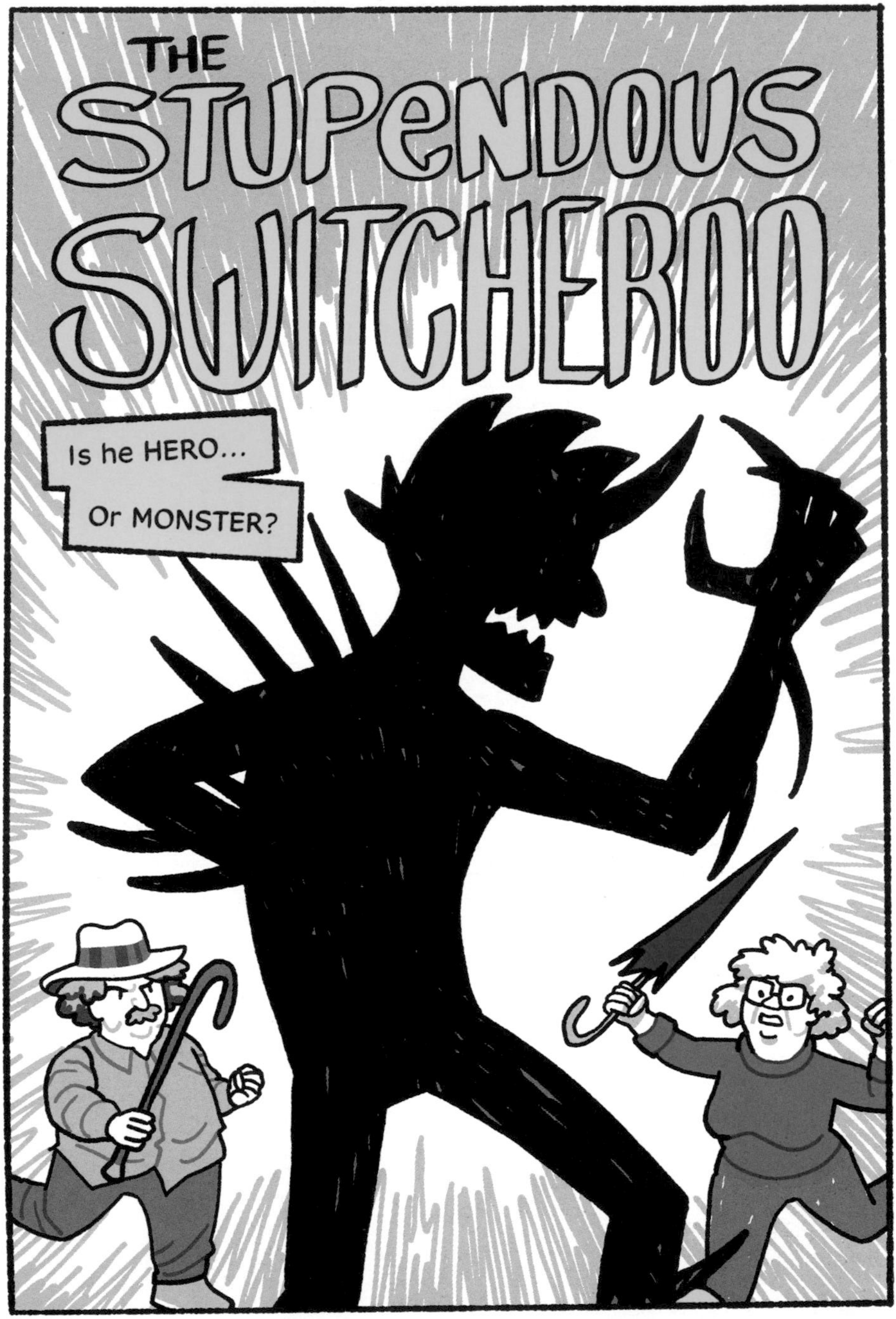
THE STUPENDOUS SWITCHEROO
Is he HERO...
Or MONSTER?

CHAPTER 8

"Monster!" somebody shouts behind me.

I run. Fast. But I'm on a tightrope between two mountains, and the wire's starting to sway. A LOT.

"Get the monster!!!" more voices yell.

I run even faster, and then I hear a roaring noise, so I look up to see what's coming. Except that the wire slips out from under me.

I lose my footing.

And I start to fall.

AHHHHH!!!

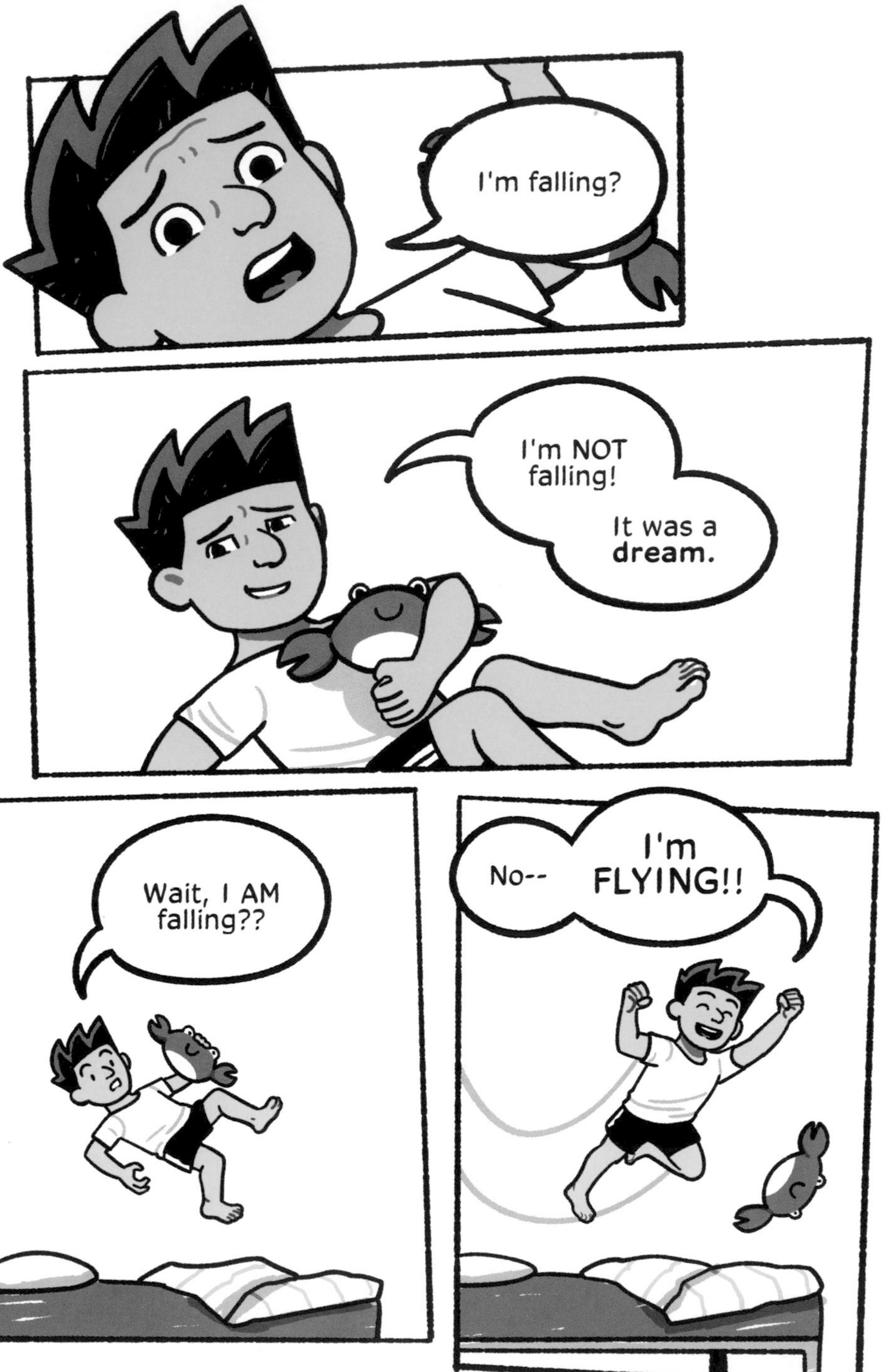

I'm falling?
I'm NOT falling!
It was a dream.
Wait, I AM falling??
No--
I'm FLYING!!

Now that I can fly, obviously I DON'T WANT TO DO ANYTHING EXCEPT FLY, so I get dressed and then swoop out of my room. (And just so you know, getting dressed is actually NOT easier when you're flying, because sometimes you're, like, wait which way is up? And then you figure it out when your underpants fall on your head.)

"What the heck?" Al says as I zoom past. "Where are you going? What about breakfast?"

"Breakfast can wait!" I say as I fly into the teleporter.

Everything is so quiet up here.

It's just me, the clouds, and a few birds who look kind of surprised.

There's been so much—SO MUCH—to worry about the last few days. Mom. My powers. Whether the tech genius superhero I've looked up to my entire life is making a terrible mistake.

It's kind of a lot.

And this is exactly what I needed! As I do gentle loop-de-loops in the air, I can feel my worries falling away.

I know, I know, all those worries will be back. And I know I told Tana I'd go check out that press conference and look for the mysterious man.

I just want this one moment.

Sooooo peaceful...

RIING RIING

RIING RIING

I absolutely do NOT hear a phone right now.

I can call Tana back later. Right now, I'm enjoying the solitude of—

Okay, okay, I'll answer the phone.

Hey, Tana--

It's not Tana, it's me, and we have a **really big problem**--

I don't know what to do or if it's already too late but they can't take him too they just can't

"Take *who*?" I ask.

"Slimeball. He's going after Vin Valor."

"He *what*??"

"He thinks it's *his* fault his dad got caught in the park that day. He'd snuck out, and his dad was trying to find him—it's why he's been so angry, and this morning, he just . . . lost it. Vin Valor's holding a press conference at the jail, some kind of grand opening ceremony—"

"I know about that, but what—"

"Slimeball went to confront Valor on live TV. There'll be cameras everywhere."

"I'll go," I say. "If you couldn't stop him, I don't think I can. But I'll try."

She gives me the coordinates, and I fly straight there. There's a crowd below, and a platform with a podium, and the enormous jail just beyond them. Something about the jail gives me the creeps.

I'm about to fly down, when I realize that if Slimeball's wearing a disguise, maybe I need one, too.

I land a few yards away, and then casually join the crowd.

I don't see Slimeball anywhere, even in disguise. I don't see Vin Valor, either, for that matter.

All around me, the crowd is growing restless waiting for the event to start.

Just then, music comes through the speakers, and Vin Valor takes the stage. Except . . . he's not alone.

Vin Valor smiles at the crowd. "I, along with the top students at the Valor Innovations Academy, want to welcome you . . ."

Too bad my power today isn't being tall—I definitely need a better view if I'm going to spot Slimeball or the mysterious man. I squeeze through the crowd, pushing my way toward the front.

"Before the ceremonial ribbon-cutting," Vin Valor continues, "I'll take any questions about ValorMax, my new, extra maximum security prison for villains—"

"Mr. Valor! Mr. Valor!" The reporters all raise their hands and yell his name—guess I'm not the only one with questions about the jail.

Well, *that* doesn't sound good.

"Switcheroo!" Tana whispers by my ear. Somehow, she snuck offstage, and now she's standing right behind me.

"Tana!" I whisper back. "How'd you get off the stage? And how'd you know it was me?"

"Any luck?" she asks.

"No mysterious man so far. But also, there's . . . a possible complication. Don't worry—I'm trying to stop it before it happens."

She nods. "Mr. Valor is finally going to let me go with him into the jail later today. That might give us some answers."

"Great," I start to say. But then something catches my eye. Something . . . slimy.

"I need to go!" I whisper. "Let me know what you find in the jail!"

"Be careful," she calls after me.

I push through the crowd, running over to Slimeball. I'm almost there . . .

. . . when he leaps onto the stage.

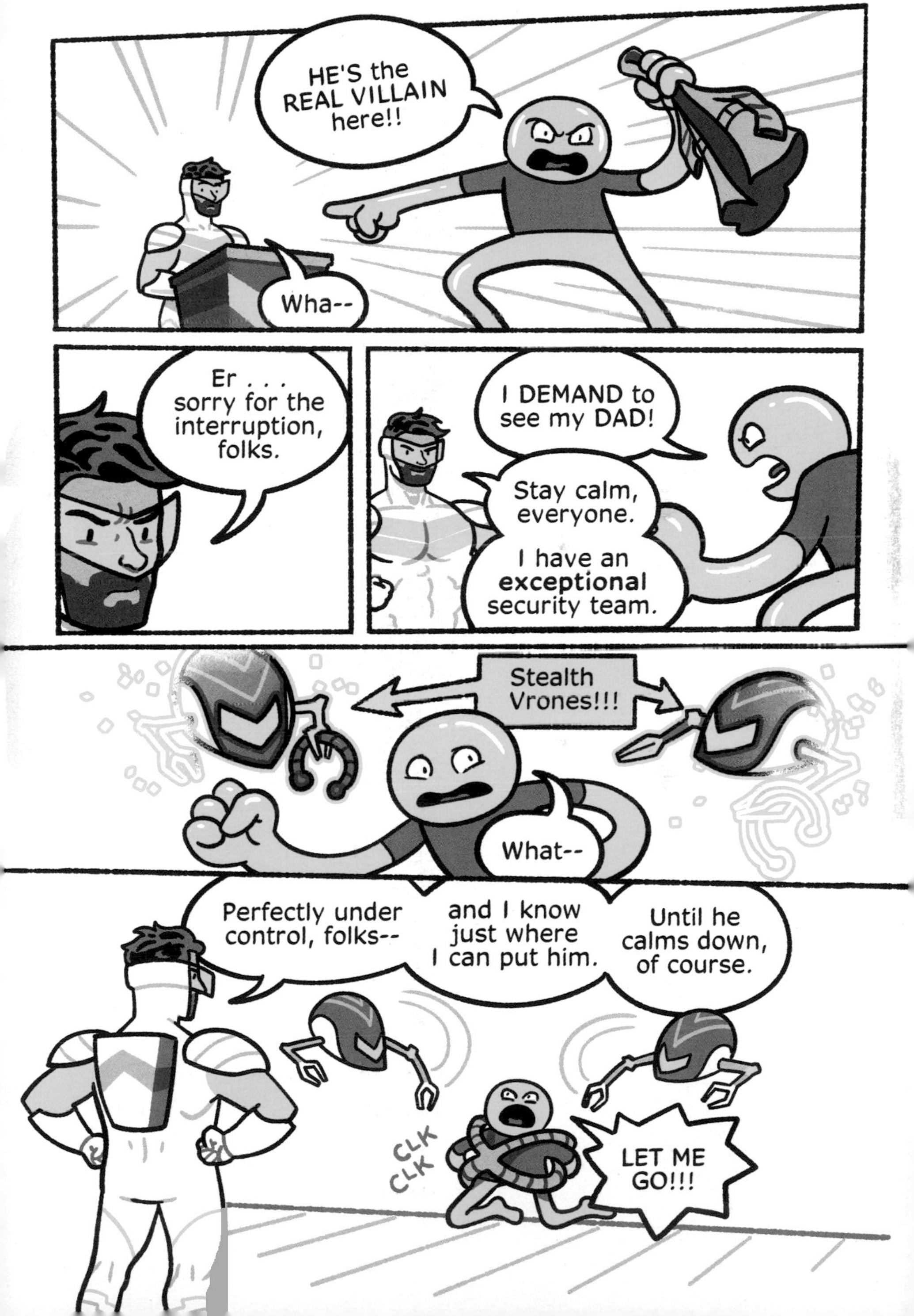
HE'S the REAL VILLAIN here!!
Wha--
Er . . . sorry for the interruption, folks.
I DEMAND to see my DAD!
Stay calm, everyone.
I have an **exceptional** security team.
Stealth Vrones!!!
What--
Perfectly under control, folks--
and I know just where I can put him.
Until he calms down, of course.
CLK CLK
LET ME GO!!!

I know exactly what I have to do. It's not great—I wanted to figure things out and *then* talk to Vin Valor about it all, and if I do this, he's going to think I'm against him, when really all I want is the truth.

But I don't have a choice. Slimeball won't be reasonable, and Vin Valor's going to end up putting him in jail.

So I'll teleport him away, like I did with Gasket.

I dive next to Slimeball and I'm just about to push the teleport button when . . .

I don't understand! We should be teleporting away by now! I look at Slimeball . . . *but he's not there anymore.* There's just a big ball of slime.

OOOOH.

We all watch, dumbfounded, as the big ball of slime that used to be Slimeball gently rolls out of the restraints.

The moment he's free, he turns back into himself and looks around at all of it: me, Vin Valor, the Vrones, the reporters. He looks . . . really freaked out.

Before he can get himself captured again, I yell, "Go! Your dad wouldn't want this!"

"It was my fault," Slimeball says, his voice cracking. "That he got caught."

"GO!" I yell.

But I don't think he hears me because the shock wears off everybody at the same time, and the Vrones start to go after him. Slimeball makes a mad dash for the middle of the street, the Vrones following in formation close behind. He gets to the storm drain and stops, looking back at me.

Cameras are flashing, and I can hear reporters yelling new questions. "Who's that kid with the mask?" "What about that slime kid?" "Are you under attack?" Vin Valor lifts me off the ground, throws an arm around me, tight. He waves at the crowd.

"No attack, just a little demonstration, folks," Vin Valor says, and they all applaud. "Why don't you all take a look at the gifts in the press kit? We even included novelty jumpsuits, just like the ones our prisoners wear!"

Then, the moment they're distracted, he turns me to face him and puts his hands on my shoulders. "I have you surrounded," he whispers. "Please don't do anything stupid."

I see Tana out of the corner of my eye. She's back on the platform again, watching us. "The thing is," I say, "there's been a huge misunderstanding. About the villains."

And I was hoping we could talk?

"This really isn't the time," he says, gesturing toward the reporters. "I have a ribbon-cutting to get back to. It's certainly disappointing to discover that you're in league with the villains. But it's not surprising."

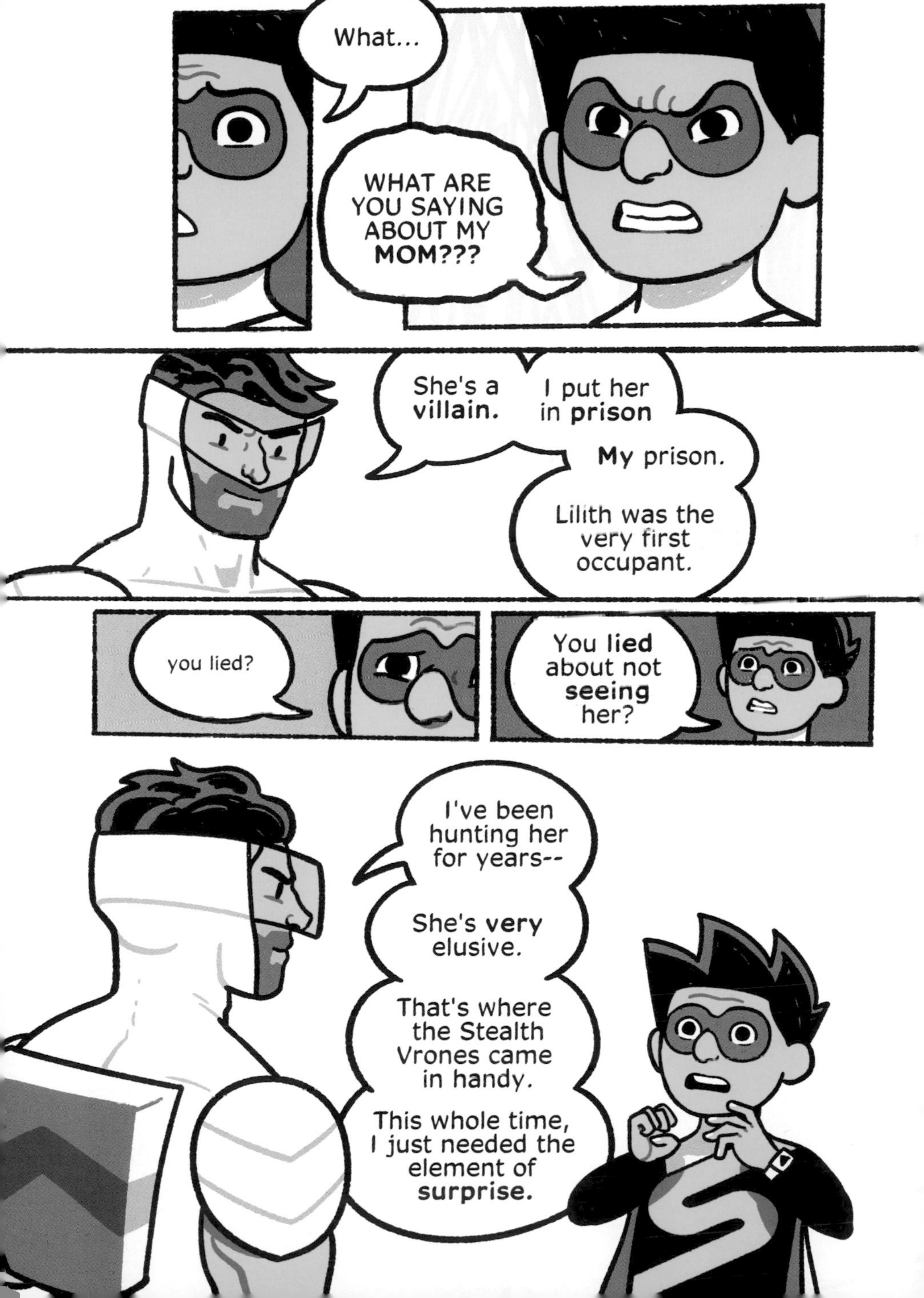
What...
WHAT ARE YOU SAYING ABOUT MY **MOM???**
She's a **villain.**
I put her in **prison**
My prison.
Lilith was the very first occupant.
you lied?
You **lied** about not **seeing** her?
I've been hunting her for years--
She's **very** elusive.
That's where the Stealth Vrones came in handy.
This whole time, I just needed the element of **surprise.**

I'm so close to Vin Valor, I wonder if he can hear everything inside me breaking to pieces. I believed him. Trusted him. Even though everything felt wrong, I didn't think my hero would lie to me.

But he did.

He lied about the most important thing in the whole world.

All I can think now is: *I need my mom.*

Good thing I can fly.

I rocket up into the air, hearing the reporters on the ground gasp—I guess they're paying attention again now. But it doesn't matter. I don't care about the press conference or the mysterious man or anything.

I just need to get to my mom.

"Let . . . me . . . go!" I yell, twisting out from under the grappling hook. It clanks onto the ground below and I fly toward the jail again, even faster than before.

I'm closing the distance when I hear a familiar sound behind me.

The roar of Vin Valor's jet pack.

I forgot I'm not the only one who can fly.

I speed up as much as I can, moving so fast I'm in danger of losing control, but a second later, Vin Valor slams into me and grabs me in a bear hug. He's pulling me back down, away from the jail, away from my mom, and even though I'm trying to get free, I know it's impossible. And he knows it, too.

I won't.

I won't ever give up.

He may be bigger and stronger and—wait.

His jets are too powerful for me to push against, but what if I reverse direction? If I change direction to go *with* him, we'll go back down faster than he's expecting.

The element of surprise.

If I have the element of surprise, maybe I can get away from him.

It's worth a shot.

I stop struggling, and for a moment, I see the triumph in his eyes. That's when I start flying down. And it works. We're suddenly plummeting, and he can't figure out what's happening, and we're going to crash right behind the platform—

Oh no.

We're going to—

Ugh...

Are you... are you okay?

What did I do?

Did I just KILL Vin Valor?

"These Vrones will escort you to the prison," Vin Valor says. "You'll get your very own room."

"Sir, do you need any help?" one of the students calls down from the platform.

"I'm fine," says Vin Valor. "This young man, however, has seen better days."

Two of the Vrones clamp onto my shoulders, hard. I can already tell there's no way I'll be able to get out from under them. My only hope now is to teleport— and at least I can reach the Pinpointer again. I push a few buttons, and for the second time, it makes a terrible FZZZT sound. And I don't go anywhere.

From the ground, Vin Valor smiles weakly.

"You can't teleport your way out of this," he says.

I stare at him. *He's* the reason I can't teleport?

"That technology shouldn't exist," he says. "It's catastrophically dangerous in the wrong hands. Namely, yours. And I may not know how to make it myself—but I've learned how to stop it."

The Vrones start to march me away, but something on the platform catches my eye.

SomeONE.

I made it.

I made it.

I can't believe I made it.

"I made you some eggs!" announces Al, rolling in. "And they are veeeery cold. You were gone considerably longer than I expected."

"It was almost a lot longer," I say.

Wait--are you okay? What happened?

I've found Mom.

But--it's bad.

I pick a little at the very cold eggs and toast while I tell Al everything.

I've just finished when I get a text.

TG Can you come get me?
AS SOON AS POSSIBLE.

Remember how I said I'd **ask** before I brought another friend over?

Is it Tana?

She *saved* you.

She's welcome here.

One minute later.

I brought a few things.

"No big deal," she says gruffly. "You'd have done the same for me."

"I would have," I agree.

"There's just one small thing," she adds. "When the other students tell Mr. Valor what I did, which is probably happening riiiiight"—she looks at her wrist thingy—"*now* . . . I'll be expelled from the Valor Innovations Academy."

"Oh no," I say. "I'm so sorry."

"It's okay," she says. "I brought my work with me. I just need a place to—"

She nods. "I understand. I'll help, whatever you decide. And maybe I can come back tomorrow morning and get to work setting up my projects?"

"If you let me look at that"—Al points to Tana's wrist thingy—"I can give you limited access to the teleporter for coming and going. If it's safe?"

"It's safe," Tana says with a smile. "I've disconnected it from the VTech network. And that's very nice of you."

It IS nice. *Suspiciously* nice.

Al sets Tana up for teleporting in and out, and then we say goodbye. The moment she's gone, I turn to Al. "Why are you being so nice suddenly? You basically had a nuclear meltdown when I brought Gasket here."

Al beeps, whirs, and then shrugs. "Everything has changed. Mom's not coming back."

"Do you believe him?" asks Al.

"No," I say slowly. "He's not the hero I thought he was. So I don't know if I can believe anything he says."

"That's a reasonable deduction," Al agrees. "Perhaps we should—"

"I need to go back out," I interrupt, picturing Mom sitting in that jail.

"But Vin Valor will be looking for you—"

"I'll go to the other side of the world," I argue. "But I need to figure this out. And flying will help me think."

It's clear Al disapproves, but I teleport out anyway, to the other side of the world, just like I said I would.

A hero would know what to do. And I always wanted to be a hero, like the ones in my comic books, like Vin Valor and the Granite Woman and Manny Mystery. When I got my powers, it felt like being part of a special club.

But the Granite Woman retired. Manny Mystery disappeared years ago. And Vin Valor's not who I thought he was. Everything's complicated. There is no special club.

Even my own mom can't help me now.

I'm going to have to figure out how to be a hero on my own.

How do I help Mom?

Why does Vin Valor want me in jail?

Who can I trust?

I fly for hours and hours and hours. I spend a lot of time thinking about those questions.

And a lot of time not even thinking at all.

THE STUPENDOUS SWITCHEROO

A HERO ON HIS OWN

CHAPTER 9

A loud knock startles me awake, and then somebody calls through the door. "Switcheroo? You in there? You're not still asleep, right? Hellooooo?"

"Um . . . what are you doing in my home?" I ask, still groggy with sleep—and then it all comes back to me. The press conference. The certain doom. The escape. "Give me three minutes."

Five minutes later, I'm dressed, my hair looks almost normal, and Mr. Meatballs, Al, and I are watching Tana unpack her equipment.

I change the subject by asking Al to scan for my power, which only takes a couple of seconds. "Thunder-hands!" Al announces, like that's a thing.

But I guess it's a thing now. So . . . I clap.

"*Very* useful," I say. "I'll clap loud enough to convince Vin Valor to let everybody out of the jail, which will work right up until he puts in earplugs."

Tana studies me for a second. "I think it doesn't matter. Whatever you decide to do next, you can't rely on your powers to save you."

Al frowns. "Isn't that the point of powers?"

"Mr. Valor has his own lab and basically an infinite amount of resources," she says. "Switcheroo can't out-*power* him. He'll have to out*smart* him."

"You can do it," Tana assures me. "And I'll help. In fact, I'm just putting the finishing touches on something that might be useful—but does your mom have a turbidimeter anywhere?"

I look at Al. Al looks at me.

"Looks sort of like a hairbrush?" Tana says.

Since Al and I have never even heard the word *turbidimeter* before, the three of us each take a cabinet and search for something that looks like a hairbrush. My cabinet is chock-full of lab equipment that looks like it might also be alien technology? My mom's work is *weird*.

MY LOST PHONE. I can't believe it. I turn it on and the screen lights up. One missed call from Mom. From ten days ago. She *did* send me a message. *I knew it.* I'm shaking as I put it on speakerphone so Al and Tana can hear.

"Sweetheart, it's me.

"I'm so sorry to leave this in a message. But I'm about to be apprehended and I won't be able to call again. Please listen carefully.

"You have a choice before you. I've instructed Al to draw a bath. The bath will give you remarkable powers. I cannot, however, predict those powers. It's too soon, my work is not yet complete.

"You are perfect the way you are. I do not need you to do this. But if he's remembered enough to come after *me*, he may come after *you*. So I want you to—"

There's a sickening crashing sound.

After the message ends, time stands still for a second. The next thing I know, Tana has dragged over a stool for me to sit on. Al is beeping worriedly.

"I'm okay," I say slowly. "I know she's alive. And it was . . . really nice to hear her voice."

After another long moment, Tana says gently, "So your powers . . . ?"

"I took the bath by accident," I say.

"You didn't even get to choose," she says quietly. "Do you . . . regret it?"

Sometimes.

"Well, to be clear, I definitely don't want to be a hero like you," she says.

"Um . . . thanks?"

"But there's different ways of being a hero. See, I was so obsessed with Valor Tech that I didn't even realize what was going on. When you first told me"— she grimaces—"part of me didn't want to leave. I've worked so hard to be the top student. And that place has everything an inventor could want."

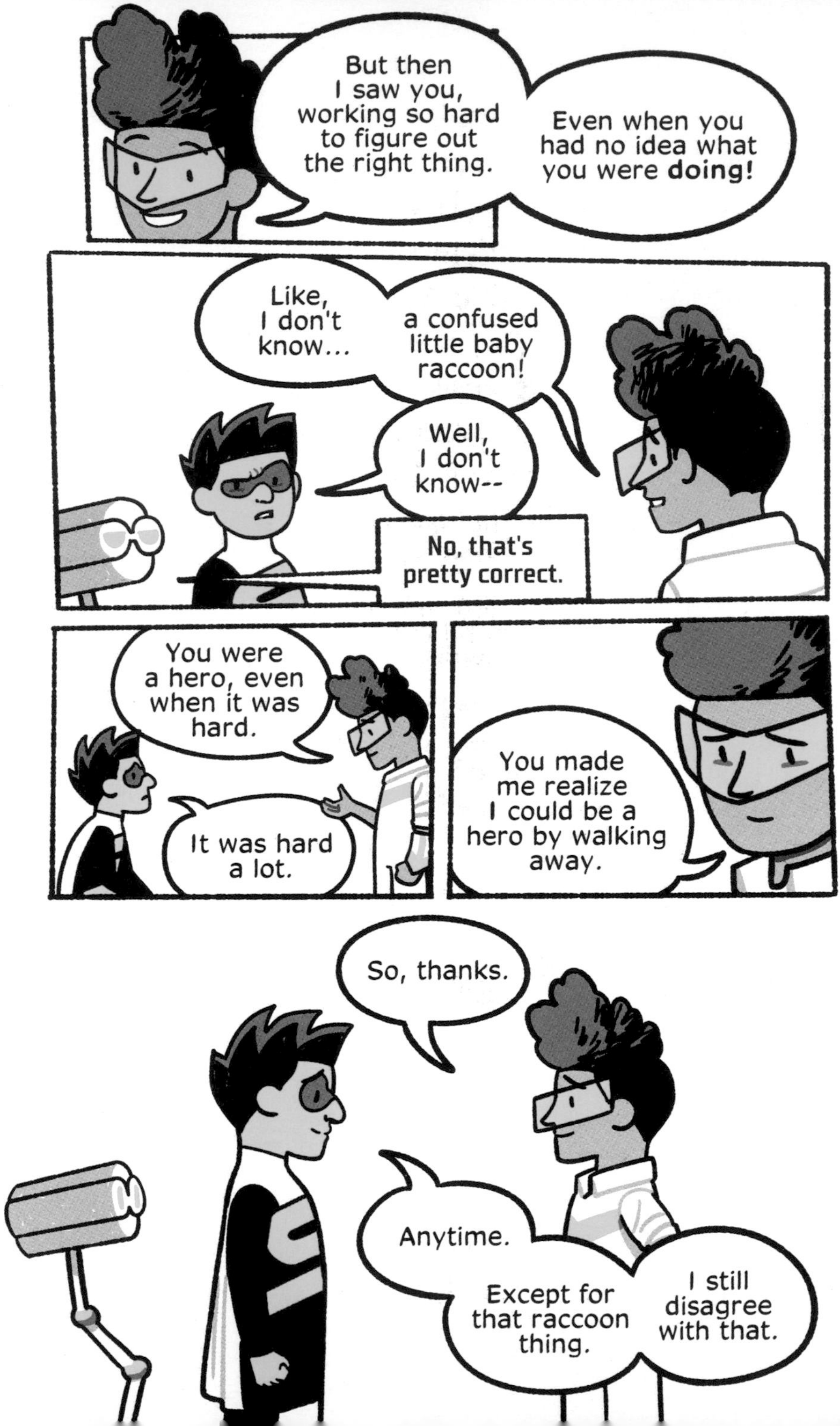
But then I saw you, working so hard to figure out the right thing.
Even when you had no idea what you were **doing!**
Like, I don't know...
a confused little baby raccoon!
Well, I don't know--
No, that's pretty correct.
You were a hero, even when it was hard.
It was hard a lot.
You made me realize I could be a hero by walking away.
So, thanks.
Anytime.
Except for that raccoon thing.
I still disagree with that.

"So," Al says. "How can we make *this* lab everything you could ever want?"

While Tana and Al talk about lab supplies, my mind wanders. Tana said I'd have to outsmart Vin Valor. The chances of me succeeding would be a lot better if I had any idea where to start.

It would help if I knew what Vin Valor was doing with all the people he captured.

"I have a theory about that," Tana says.

I . . . guess I said that last part out loud.

"I think he's studying their powers. And how their powers work. How they GOT their powers, too."

My heart is suddenly racing. "Tana . . . my *MOM* was studying them. She had files on all of them in the secret lab, let me show you—"

Al makes a long, pleading sort of bleep.

"What?" I say. "You're the one who said everything was different now. You were right."

I show Tana how the entrance works, and she gasps as the door opens.

I point out the file cabinets and all of Mom's detailed notes on the villains. "So . . . that's the secret lab," I say. "Except I think we need a new name for it. The time for secrets is over."

It's incredible.

It's like a **bank vault.**

Except instead of money, it's filled with research on villains.

That's it!

We'll call it **The Vault.**

"I'm not sure where to start," I admit. But this feels like it could be a breakthrough—and the faster we can figure out how my mom and Vin Valor and the villains are all tangled up, the better.

Tana begins poring over the files. "Mr. Valor has a little information on some of the villains, but nothing like this. I mean, who would have guessed that Mr. Sucko's first name was Todd?"

Suddenly, my pocket buzzes. It's the VTech phone—
and there's a text from an unknown number.

> **?** We need to meet. The usual place.

Then another text comes through.

> **?** This is Gasket.

Before I can type a response, I get a *two more* texts.

> **?** DO NOT TELL YOUR ROBOT.

> **?** DO NOT TELL ANYONE.

"News?" Tana asks, startling me.
"Oh, um, I need to . . . run an errand."

"Fine. It's Gasket," I explain. "But I'm not supposed to tell you."

"I understand," says Tana, pretending to lock her mouth and throw away the key.

"You're okay here?" I ask.

She nods. "I'll keep going through these files. Maybe I can figure out what your mom was doing with them."

Al offers to help (which *would* be nice, except I'm guessing it's mostly to make sure Tana doesn't blow anything up), so they get to work while I head to the teleporter.

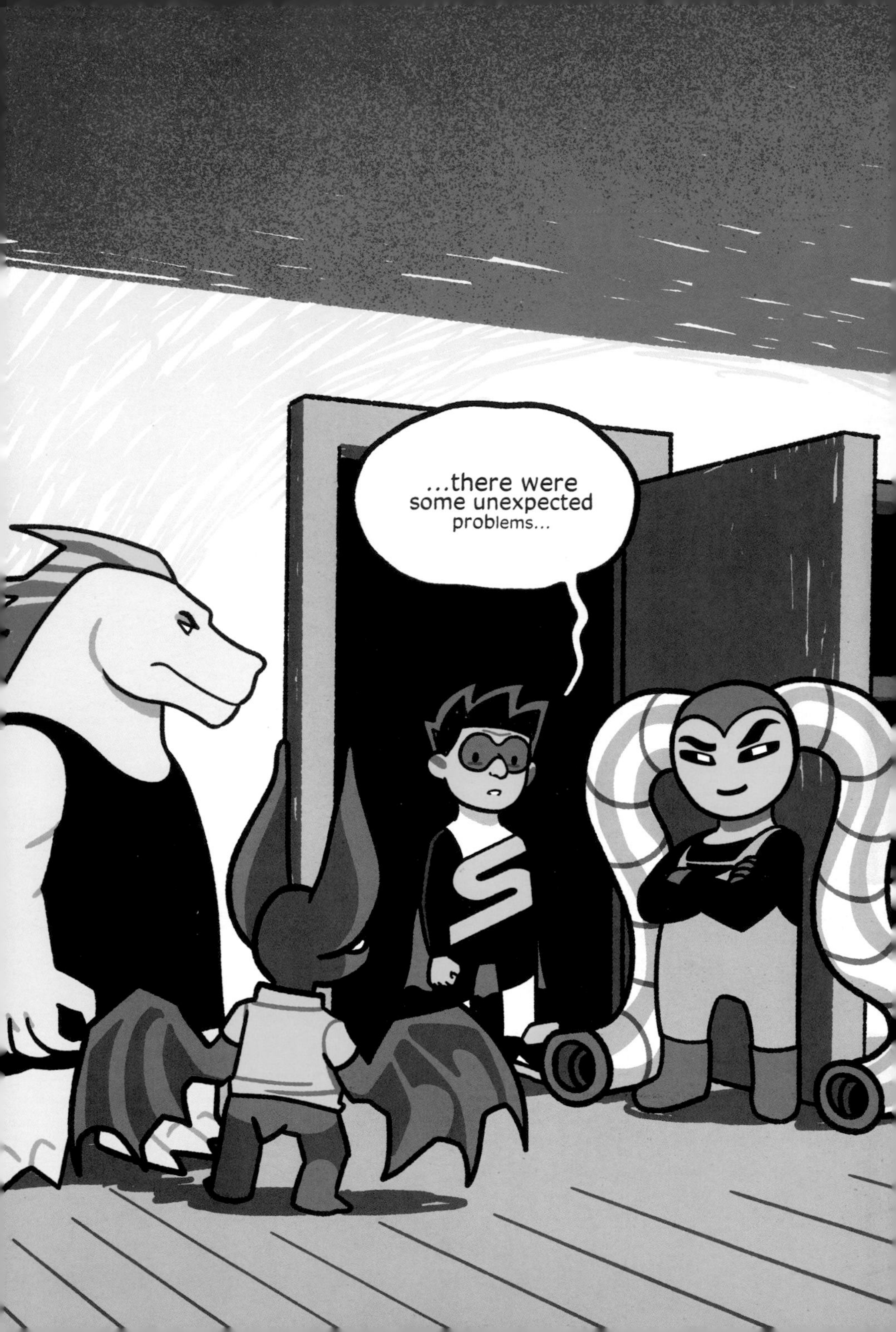
...there were some unexpected problems...

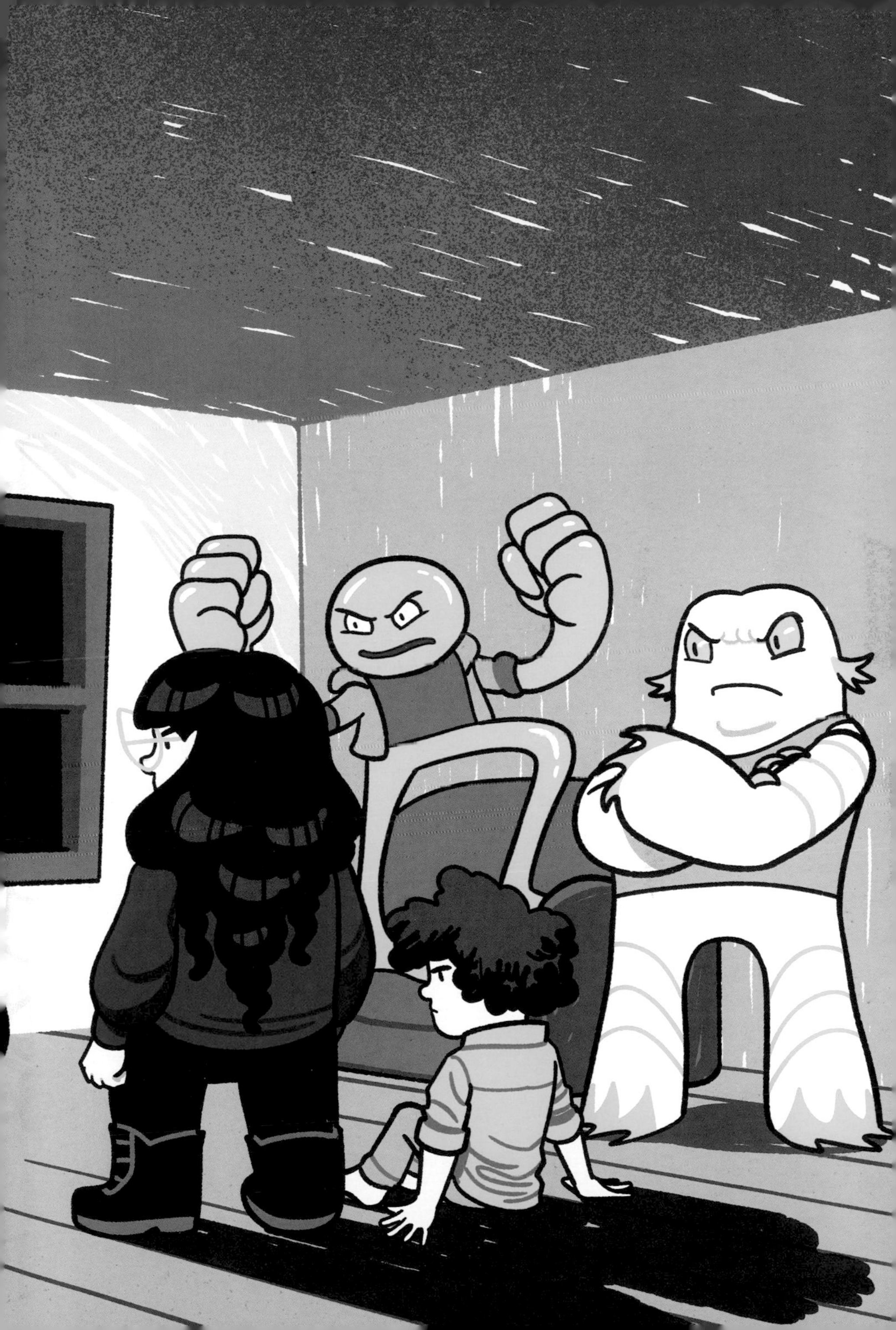

They all look at me for a second. And then the room explodes in conversation.

"Clam it!" yells Gasket, and everybody goes quiet.

"I think you mean clam UP," says the little kid, but the girl next to him shushes him.

"This is Switch," says Gasket.

"And this is Switch's phone," says Slimeball, holding up my VTech phone.

"How'd you get that?" I ask as Slimeball drops it to the ground and stomps on it. "Hey! Don't smash my—"

"It's VTech," he interrupts me. "They'll track the phone as soon as they remember you have it. Maybe they already have."

Ugh. He's right.

You have to get used to thinking of yourself as **the enemy.**

"But I'm *not* the enemy," I protest.

"Oh, you're *somebody's* enemy—you just have to decide whose," says the kid with the bat wings.

"And you have to decide tonight," says Slimeball.

Gasket clears her throat. "We figured it was time for you to meet the rest of the fake Vin Valor #1 Fan Club."

"Um . . . hi there," I say. "Very nice to meet you."

"He'll have a different power tomorrow," Gasket reminds everybody.

"He better," mutters Komoda.

"It'll be a different power, but it might not be more useful," I add, and I can instantly tell that does not improve everybody's opinion of me. "Tana says that whatever plan we come up with—"

"WHO'S TANA?" asks Slimeball.

"Oh," I say. "Right."

Gasket holds her face in her hands. "Please tell me you aren't still in touch with your little VTech friend."

"Actually, she's at my house right now—"

And like before, every one of them starts talking again. *This* time, I decide to take matters into my own hands. Literally.

You gotta be kidding.

BUGS!

Where???

She's a spy!

HE'S a spy!!

...can't be trusted...

BOOM!!

Like I said.

Pretty loud.

"I get it," I say. "But *Tana's* the one who kept me from going to jail after Slimeball oozed himself down that drain, and now she's been kicked out of the Innovations Academy for smashing equipment and helping me. *She's on our side.* And she's awesome. Why can't we all work together?"

For a second, none of them say anything. Then Bugsy shrugs and says, "Anybody who's been kicked out of Vin Valor's school sounds good to me."

"Don't forget that she smashed stuff," adds Komoda. "I like that quality in a person."

"*Everybody we know* smashes stuff. That doesn't mean anything," Tooter argues. "And we shouldn't have invited *him* here to begin with."

"He's dangerous," Trip says quietly.

"Let's take a vote," says Gasket.

Do We Trust Switcheroo??

YES   NO

"Slimeball?" asks Gasket.

"I'm undecided," Slimeball says. "I mean, he did come to help me. On the other hand, he's sort of a weirdo."

I'm not sure how I feel about being called a weirdo by a kid who turns into a literal ball of slime.

"Also," says Bugsy, "Bobby's vote doesn't count."

"It's not fair to throw out my vote just because I'm the youngest," Bobby huffs.

"That's not why," says Bugsy, rolling his eyes. "It's because you always vote no to everything."

I have a bad feeling about this. "Who is your—"

"Trip is just my nickname," Trip says sadly. "Because I'm the third. The triple. I'm the Shadow's Shadow's Shadow."

I gasp. When I finally speak, my voice shakes. "I had no idea the blue luxolyte would do that. I'm so sorry. I'd take it back if I could."

"Dad would be free if it weren't for you," Bobby says. "Vin Valor said so himself in the report."

"Wait a minute. How . . . how did you read Vin Valor's report?" I ask.

Bobby glances at Gasket and the room goes still. I don't understand what's happening, but I don't like it.

"Your mom's name is Lilith, right?" Gasket says slowly. "How much do you know about her?"

What?

I know everything about my mom. I know that she thinks knock-knock jokes are hilarious. I know that she loves birthdays. And that she forgets that socks should match. I know she loves me.

But then I think about those files in The Vault.

And about what Vin Valor said.

About the message she left.

I don't know anything about my mom.

Tell me.

"I found records," Gasket says. "Notes about experiments that happened before any of us were born. The experiments that turned our parents into freaks and gave them powers that scared people."

"Those experiments happened at Valor Technologies?" I ask, trying to make sense of it.

"That's where they *started*," Gasket says. "But the lead scientist decided she didn't want Valor Tech to have the technology. Late one night, when no one else was working, she took all the research and left."

The lead scientist was your mom.

My mind is spinning. She can't be right. That's impossible. Because that would mean . . .

. . . my mom created every single supervillain.

"It doesn't make sense," I start to say, but then I realize it makes *total* sense. It explains all those files in The Vault.

"She was the mastermind," Gasket confirms. "And then she destroyed all the evidence. I mean ALL the evidence. Our parents have never been able to tell us what happened to them."

My heart is racing. Because she *didn't* destroy everything. Not the stuff in The Vault, anyway. There are stacks and stacks of pages, full of details. And I'm about to say so when Bugsy adds, "And it's not like she didn't have plenty of opportunities to tell us."

"And Dr. L was . . . *my mom*? This whole time?" I ask. "How long have you known?"

Gasket shrugs. "I started getting curious when you showed up using a teleporter. And then you asked me to track her hovercar—average people don't just have those."

"Oh. Right." I guess there's really nothing average about my mom.

"We've lived in a hidden-away neighborhood our entire lives," Gasket continues. "It's just down the hill from here. Dr. L used to bring us things we needed, so nobody had to risk going out into the world and getting arrested at the grocery store."

"Do you know how embarrassing it is to get accused of being a villain when you're just trying to buy toilet paper?" asks Slimeball.

Gasket nods. "Dr. L's visits stopped around the same time your mom vanished. We've had to take care of things ourselves."

I want to hear more about all of this, about where they live, and what else my mom does that I don't know about. But something's still bugging me. "What does any of this have to do with Vin Valor?"

"Good question," Gasket says. "According to the notes I found, Vin Valor's been obsessed with figuring out what happened. It's taken him years to uncover this much. I still can't figure out how she did such a good job of hiding everything she did."

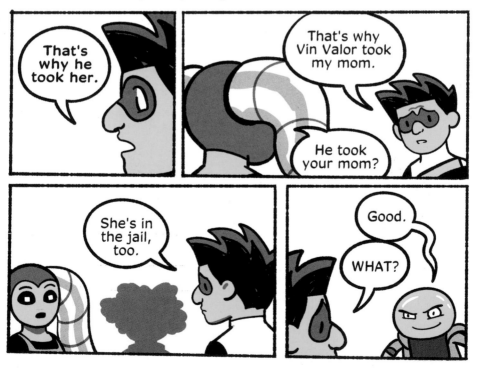

Gasket tells everybody to be quiet, and then turns to me.

"We have a plan," she says. "But we need your help. And now you have a pretty good reason to help us."

"I don't think Vin Valor's going to listen to me. I already tried talking to him—"

We aren't going to **talk** to him.

We're doing a **jailbreak**.

You brought me here to **blackmail** me into helping you--

We didn't think you'd want it getting out that your mom is the biggest supervillain of all.

But since your mom is in there, too...

It's gonna be great.

We're getting our parents out--

Except it's **totally** not going to work.

BOBBY!!!

Hmph.

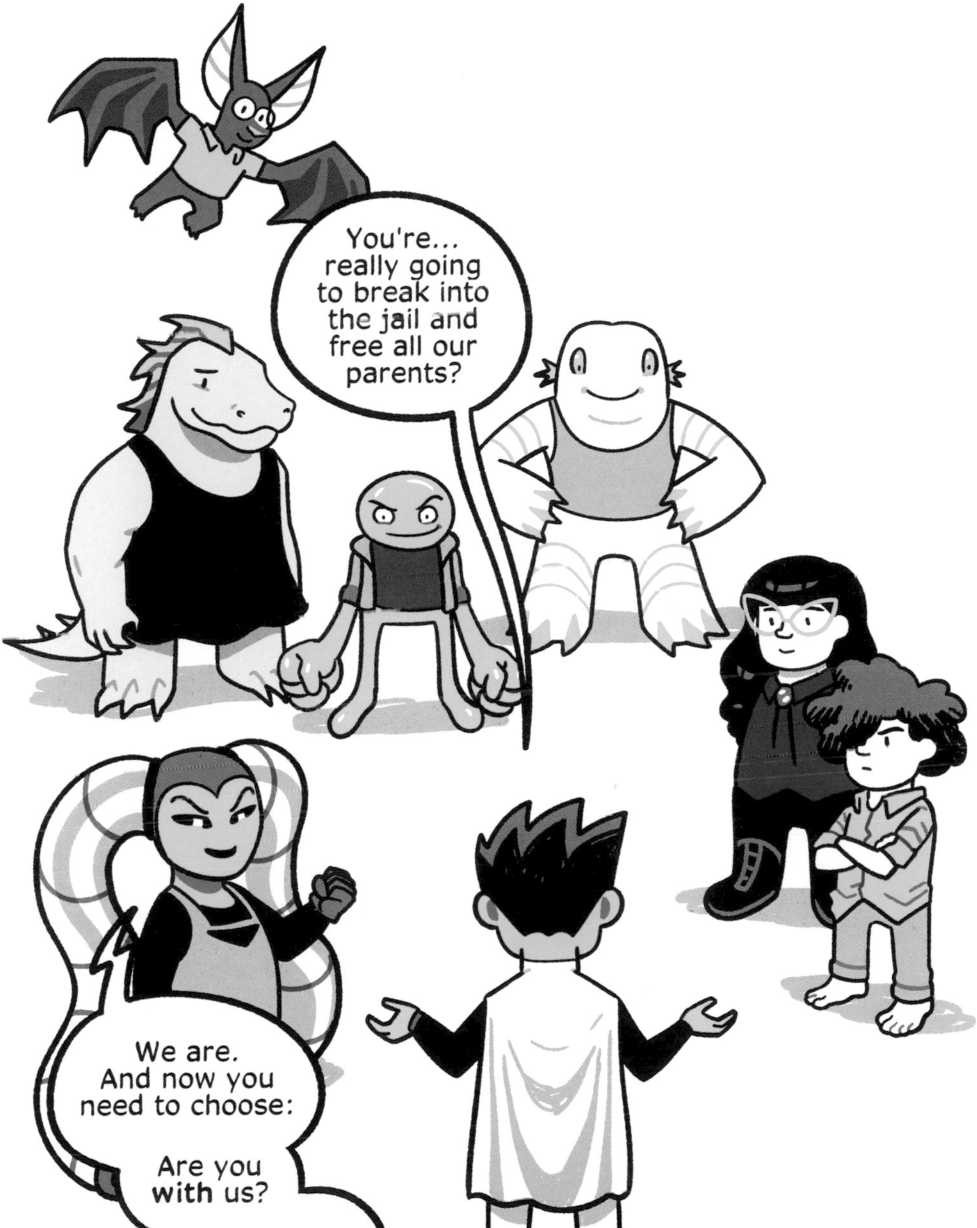
You're... really going to break into the jail and free all our parents?
We are. And now you need to choose:
Are you **with** us?
Or **against** us?

I don't know what to say. I'm not a person who breaks into jails. I'm a hero. At least, I THOUGHT I was a hero.

But I've been wrong about so much. Maybe the jail is wrong. Maybe everybody has a secret. Maybe heroes don't exist.

What do I know for sure?

I know that my mom is in jail, and I want to get her out.

The moment I say the words, a couple of them cheer. Komoda hugs me so hard I think my bones are going to break, and even Trip gives a half-smile. Suddenly, they aren't a club of junior supervillains. They're just a bunch of relieved kids.

But in my head, it's still sinking in. Am I really going to help them break our parents out of jail?

Yeah.

I really am.

I guess that means I'm going to be a **supervillain.**

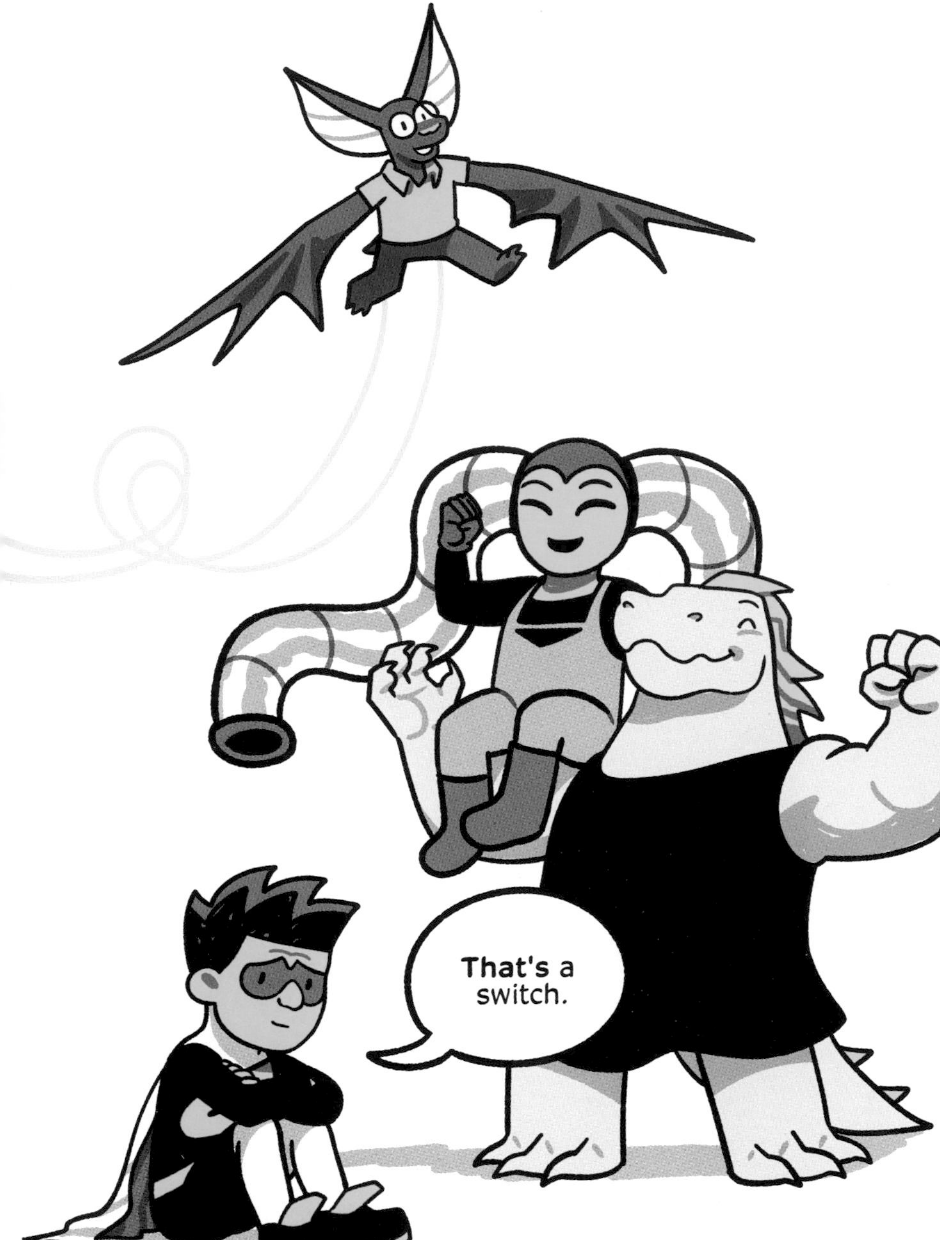
That's a switch.

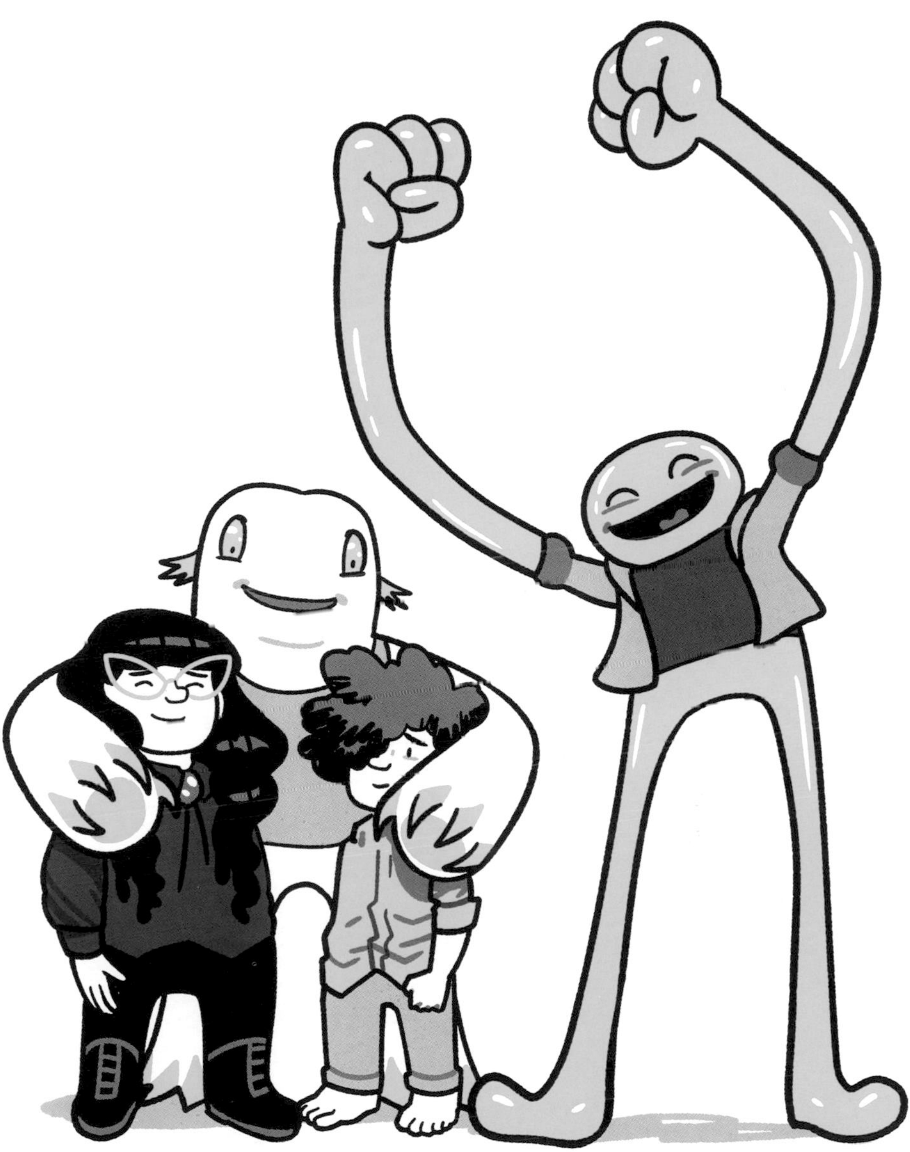

THE STUPENDOUS SWITCHEROO

Volume 2

Born to Be Bad

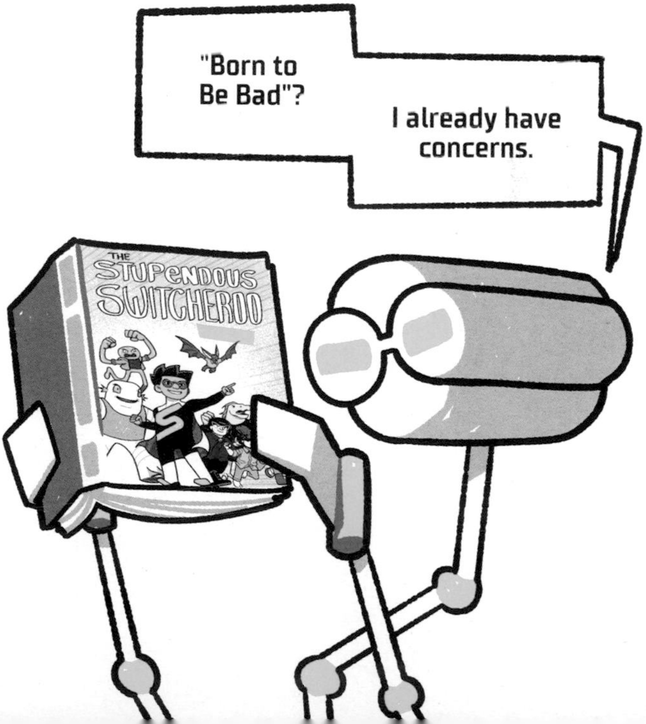

"Born to
Be Bad"?
I already have
concerns.
THE STUPENDOUS SWITCHEROO

A NOTE FROM THE CREATORS

In early March 2020, Chad and Mary Winn went on a walk around their Chicago neighborhood.

Chad had a really cool idea for a story about a kid with a different superpower every day, and he asked Mary Winn if she wanted to tell the story with him. She was all in.

There was only one problem: they'd decided to write the story at the exact same time the pandemic hit.

So, at first, they talked about it online, even though they only lived seventeen houses apart.

When it was okay to go on walks again, they went on walks. They talked for hours and hours about this sweet, funny kid and all his bonkers powers.

Having something to dream about together made the tough times a little brighter.

This is a shout-out to friends and dreams and all of us helping each other through difficult times. It's exactly the sort of thing the Stupendous Switcheroo would do.

MARY WINN HEIDER'S

other books include *The Mortification of Fovea Munson* and *The Losers at the Center of the Galaxy*. Along with composer Justin Huertas, Mary Winn also co-wrote a musical version of *Fovea*, which has a surprising number of singing zombie frogs in it! She changes her mind a lot,  but if she could have a superpower *right now*, it would be to play every musical instrument. Mary Winn lives in Chicago with one husband, one ~~intern~~ cat, and eleven billion books.

CHAD SELL

is a lifelong lover of super-hero comics and movies. He has worked on two graphic novel series for children, The Cardboard Kingdom and Doodleville. Chad co-writes and illustrates the Card-board Kingdom with a team of collaborators, and he is  the sole creator of Doodleville. If he had a superpower, Chad would like the ability to talk with animals. Chad lives in Connecticut with his husband and cat.

ACKNOWLEDGMENTS

It takes a lot of superheroes to make a book happen!

Tammy Swinford-Potts introduced us to each other at Illinois Reads in 2019, and we'll forever be grateful to her for being the first domino in our friendship and our work together.

We are also so grateful for the incredible team at PRH/Knopf who worked on making every aspect of the Stupendous Switcheroo fantastic: the incomparable Michelle Cunningham, who designed the heck out of this book, April Ward, Jake Eldred, Claribel Vasquez, Artie Bennett, and Tamar Schwartz.

We're pretty sure that our editor, Marisa DiNovis, has *actual* editing superpowers. Thank you, Marisa, for being an original member of the #1 Switcheroo Fan Club. We're so lucky to be on this adventure with you!

As ever, we are greatly indebted to our agents, Tina Dubois and Dan Lazar. Thank you both for always keeping everything running smoothly in the author-cave! (Like the batcave? No? It's okay, they get it.)

Thanks to our friends and family. You are all the best.

Also, we had a whole team of cats who were extremely *not* helpful, but we'd like to thank them anyway. Thanks a bunch, Edie, Ivy, Monty, and Bangor.